King of the Asheville Coven

(Winterset Coven, Book 1)

&

Second of the Winterset Coven

(Winterset Coven, Book 2)

T. S. JOYCE

King of the Asheville Coven
Second of the Winterset Coven

ISBN-13: 978-1977720658
ISBN-10: 197772065X

First electronic publication: July 2016

T. S. Joyce
www. tsjoyce.com

NOTE FROM THE AUTHOR:

This book is a work of fiction. The names, characters, places, and incidents are products of the writer's imagination or have been used fictitiously and are not to be construed as real. Any resemblance to persons, living or dead, actual events, locale or organizations is entirely coincidental. The author does not have any control over and does not assume any responsibility for third-party websites or their content.

Published in the United States of America

First digital publication: July 2016
First print publication: September 2017

DEDICATION

For those of you working that night shift.
Hey there, fellow vamps.
This one's for you.

ACKNOWLEDGMENTS

I couldn't write these books without some amazing people behind me. A huge thanks to Corinne DeMaagd, for helping me to polish my books, and for being an amazing and supportive friend. Looking back on our journey here, it makes me smile so big. You are an incredible teammate, C!

And thank you, Awesome Reader. You have done more for me and my stories than I can even explain on this teeny page. You found my books, and ran with them, and every share, review, and comment makes release days so incredibly special to me.

1010 is magic and so are you.

ONE

"All units, automobile accident, ninety-two and Quail Ridge." The voice over the intercom called over the alarm.

"About time," Aric Teague muttered as he threw his crappy poker hand down on the table and jogged after the other two firefighters on shift tonight.

Chief Lang was already in the turn-out room handing out gear. Aric readied in a daze, his muscle memory remembering everything he needed to without much mental attention. His head was somewhere else. It was already on the automobile accident on ninety-second and Quail Ridge.

Dressed in the heavy gear, he bolted for the passenger's side of the fire engine. He pulled himself up, only to be yanked back down. “You’re the new guy on the truck, *vamp*,” John ground out. “Get in the back.”

Vamp. Aric barely had resisted the urge to crawl into the asshole’s mind and make him piss himself when John shoved him roughly toward where Nick was climbing in the back of the truck.

He missed Asheville.

With a low hiss in his throat, Aric climbed in the back and ignored Nick’s dirty look and muttered curses. As Chief hit the gas and turned onto West Court Avenue, Aric busied himself making sure his radio was working and his gear was fastened. John bitched on and on about why Chief had approved a supernatural for the house.

“Because we have to consider all applications, John.”

“So it’s fair that he gets to only work night shifts, while we have to work twenty-four-hour shifts away from our families?”

“He might have a family, too, and supes work different than us.” Chief Lang was being overly patient. Aric’s last fire chief would’ve told John to get over it and quit whining already. Aric got it, though.

He was new to the house, and he'd shaken up a routine they had all been used to.

"And when he gets hungry during a call? When he sees the blood and goes on a killing spree? He probably eats little babies—"

"Enough!" Aric yelled, fury blasting through his veins. "I'm fine on calls. I've worked this job for a decade and have never tasted a drop of any of the victims. Go do your fucking research online and keep your pissing and moaning to yourself. And no, I don't have a family. I have a coven under me. Tread lightly with how you talk to me."

"You're a king?" Chief asked carefully over the blaring of the sirens. "You should've told me that on your application."

"What difference does it make?" Aric added darkly as he watched the small town of Winterset blur by the window. "You and I both know you had to hire me."

And it was true. Twenty-five years ago, shifters came out to the public and fought for their rights. Vampires came out soon after. Supes, as the humans liked to call them, had to be considered for the same jobs as humans now. Aric got through the door of the

Winterset Fire Department based on *what* he was. Now he had to prove he was an asset to this truck by showing his crew *who* he was.

God, he missed his old life. He missed the Bryson City Fire Department and the guys he had worked with there. He missed the way his coven used to be before he had to force his people to flee the wrath of the Bloodrunner Crew.

As long as he lived, he would never put his coven in danger from another crew of shifters again. He winced as he rubbed his forearm, still sore from his last encounter with Harper Keller, the Bloodrunner Dragon. She'd shoved his arm in the sunlight and threatened to wage war on all vampires. Crazy fire-breather probably would've done it too. He should've killed her and claimed all her territory.

Instead he was in fucking Nowheresville, Iowa with a pissed-off coven under him and an acute hatred for these ball-busting idiots on the truck.

A police cruiser was already on the scene up ahead, and Aric muttered a curse when he got his first glance at the wreckage. The older model, black SUV had careened off into a deep ditch and was on its side. Beyond, there was only darkness, which meant the car was being propped up by something he couldn't see from here. It must've rolled because the driver's side door was caved in and a mess of metal.

"Jaws of life…" John was saying into the radio, but Aric was already bolting from the truck. The smoke billowing from the engine said they didn't have that much time.

"Help me!" the police officer yelled. "Hurry!" He was standing on the toppled SUV, straining against the door.

Shit. Aric slid down the steep ditch, dislodging leaves and earth as he went. The others were yelling behind him, but fuck it. They could get their equipment. Aric had something better.

He began to climb onto the SUV, but it rocked dangerously backward. Too much weight. "Get off!" he ordered the officer. "We can't both be up there, or it'll start rolling again.

"It's only propped up by a couple of trees," he said as he climbed down, his face pouring with sweat. "Just saplings holding her up."

Her. Damn, he hated when he lost women and children. *Stop it. She could still pull through. You haven't even seen her yet.*

One look inside the shattered window, though, and his heart dropped to the ground. He'd been able to smell the blood from the fire truck, but seeing the gore was a different story. Her hair was such a light shade of blond, it almost looked silver. Her long tresses were curled on the ends, and she wore a dress as though she'd been going somewhere nice. She was completely limp, held in the driver's seat by only her seatbelt.

"Ma'am, can you hear me?" Aric asked, reaching in to check her pulse. It was there, but too fast and too faint. He searched the mangled door for a week spot he could bully into opening. "If you can hear me, my name is Aric, and I'm with the Winterset Fire Department. We're going to get you out of here."

Smoke thickened the air, and the SUV heaved backward and settled again. He could see it now, the deep ravine below. It had been veiled in darkness, but the boys were now shining lights on the wreckage, illuminating the entire scene. He didn't mind heights and would survive, but this woman? No chance in hell if he couldn't pull her out in time.

Gritting his teeth, Aric pulled on the door. It groaned and gave a little, but not even his supernatural strength could pry it open. "Where's the jaws of life!" he yelled over his shoulder. Fuckin' humans taking too long.

The smell of gas and blood and smoke was dizzying, and the SUV leaned again with a groan of metal. The snapping of a tree sounded. The officer on the ground held onto the sidestep of the car, legs locked against the uneven footing as he tried to keep it steady.

Aric strained against the door, pulling until his muscles burned and felt like they would snap in half. His skin was tough, but his hands were bleeding from prying the jagged edges of the door.

He could hear them now, the crew. They were securing ropes onto the SUV to steady it from above, but it wouldn't save her from the fire that had sparked to life in the front of the vehicle. John had an extinguisher on it already, but couldn't get under the hood at this angle, and that's where the real problem would be.

This woman had just run out of time. "Shit," Aric muttered, unfastening his turnout gear.

"What are you doing?" John screamed.

No time to explain he couldn't shift in clothes this

heavy, he yelled, "Get back!"

One of the ropes snapped, and the backend of the SUV rotated down the hill. There was pandemonium behind him from the others, but Aric couldn't pay attention to that now. The flames up front were getting worse, and he could feel the heat radiating from the interior now. He couldn't do it. Couldn't watch this woman burn alive, couldn't watch her roll to her death in this car, couldn't lose another. Every lost life stayed with him, wrecked his dreams, made his eternity hellish. He kicked out of his fire resistant gear, reached inside the window, pulled her seatbelt to his lips, and bit through. One down. He had the belt on her lap to go before he could free her.

"Aric, it's going!" John yelled.

He could feel the exact moment the rope gave. The exact moment the fire blazed up and consumed the hood. The woman lay there limp, her arm in his grip. He had to commit fully to the pain if he wanted to get her out.

Everything slowed as the SUV rolled.

Aric dove forward, pulled the belt off her lap, and bit it as hard as he could. The trees below were coming toward the window fast, and one branch through his chest could be his final death. He wasn't ready. Wasn't ready to die, but wasn't ready to watch this stranger die either. She smelled good. Blood and something more that sang to him like a siren song. *Can't lose her.*

When she slipped free of the belt, he grabbed her waist and pulled with all his strength. There was no more time. They were both about to be crushed. Flames reached for her as Aric pulled her body through the shattered window, and bunching his muscles, he blasted upward, giving his body to the bats and smoke that were always there for him. His body shattered, but he held on to the woman. Held on as the flames exploded toward them, held on as he went airborne with her. The bats and smoke were hard to control, contorting this way and that, but always around him, around his center, around the part of him that still felt like it existed.

He lowered to the street below and landed hard. His boots caved in the concrete where they hit, but he wasn't done yet. She wasn't saved. So much blood. Smelled so good. *Stop it.*

Aric laid her down gently and pulled himself together, morphed into his fully human form again.

The crew was yelling about something below, and he could make out the glow of a raging fire over the ledge of the ravine, but Aric didn't care about that right now. He checked her pulse. Way too faint, worse than it was before.

She was losing too much blood, and he could only guess at her internal injuries. "I need a C-Collar and a board!" he yelled at Chief Lang, but the statuesque man with the gray, animated brows was staring at Aric in revulsion, completely frozen where he stood holding a radio to his lips.

His shifted form did that to people. It was probably the bats.

"Chief!"

"C-collar," the man said on a breath, seeming to come back to life.

Aric had all the paramedic certifications and knew what to do, but for some reason, this woman under his probing hands felt different. She felt important. He couldn't explain it, but if he lost her here, right now, it would hurt him.

He had to find out where her bleeding was coming from. Had to stop it so he could buy time to get her to survive the ambulance ride. In a rush, Aric ripped off her tattered dress and wiped the dark fabric over the deep gashes in her chest. The blood washed away, but no new crimson welled up in the cuts. What the hell?

Aric leaned closer and studied the pink of the muscle cinching itself up. This woman had accelerated healing. Shocked, Aric eased back and studied her face. She was beautiful with long, snow-white blond hair, skin as smooth as a polished eggshell, pert nose, full lips, and perfectly arched eyebrows just a few shades darker than her hair.

Suddenly, the woman gasped, her back arching against the asphalt, and instinctively Aric cradled her shoulders. It was then that he smelled it through the fog of blood. Fur.

Her eyes opened, and Aric had to force himself not to blast backward in defense. Her irises were a blazing gold, becoming brighter and brighter as her pupils constricted and focused on him.

No, no, no, there were no shifters in Winterset. There weren't! He had checked, and no crews were registered to this area, so why the fuck was he here, in the dead of night, hugging an obvious apex predator shifter to his chest?

She panted too fast, too shallow. She was going to pass out soon. At the sound of Chief Lang's boots approaching behind Aric, her eyes widened with fear.

"Please," she whispered.

"Please what?" Aric asked.

"Please don't tell them what I am." A long, soft breath escaped her lips, and then her eyes rolled closed as she went limp again.

Stunned, Aric dragged his gaze down the curves of her body, then back up to her face.

She hadn't come up as registered because she wasn't.

This shifter was rogue, and she'd just asked him to cover for her.

TWO

Sadey Lowen winced at the soreness in her body. She peeked her eyes open and grimaced at the brightness of the fluorescent lighting and, for a moment, couldn't figure out where she was. A high-pitched *beep, beep* prickled her oversensitive ears. One look at the monitors she was hooked up to, and she panicked. What was she doing in a hospital room?

"You don't want to report her because she's human, just like you," a low timbre said.

Sadey jerked her attention to the window dividing her room from a sterile looking hallway. Right outside stood a man who brought everything crashing back to her. The truck that had chased her down and driven her off the road, the fear, the pain, and then waking up to that man hugging her. She wouldn't have known he was supernatural, but his eyes had changed color right in front of her, from a soft gray hue to demon-black in an instant. He wasn't a shifter; she hadn't smelled fur or feathers on him, but once he'd opened his mouth to speak, his canine teeth removed any further doubt of what he was. They were too sharp, and long. A vampire.

She should've been terrified of him because she knew the terrible strength and heartlessness vamps were capable of. But in a panic not to be found out, she'd pleaded for his help instead.

Propped up on the bed, she canted her head and studied him as he talked low to a nurse outside her room. He struck a handsome profile, with eyebrows the same chestnut color as his mussed, stylish hair. His jaw was clean-shaven and chiseled, and his lips too sensual for his own damn good. His nose was straight and strong, his neck thick and muscular. His defined pecs pressed attractively against the thin material of a navy T-shirt, and she could just make out his arms as he rested his hands on his hips in what looked like an irritated gesture. Tattoos stretched from below his short sleeve to his elbow, all black ink in swirling symbols she couldn't quiet decipher, but that wasn't what tripped up her gaze. On his forearm, there was a perfect line that divided the pale skin of his upper arm from the red, raw skin that covered his elbow down. Vampires healed as fast as shifters, but this injury looked as if he'd had to regrow the skin that had been fileted off. Maybe he'd exposed it to sunlight or something.

She swallowed hard at how painful that must've been, and then a wave of guilt washed over her because perhaps it was a new burn, and maybe he'd gotten that saving her tonight.

The nurse walked in, followed by the vamp, who crossed his arms and stood against the wall. He avoided Sadey's gaze. Even from all the way over here, she could feel the heavy power he emanated. There was no doubt in her mind he could off her in an instant. Maybe that's why he was here. Vamps liked drinking shifters. Rumor had it she tasted better to the undead. Maybe he was here to make a meal of her when she was released.

The nurse, Jody, her nametag read, had a strange, vacant look on her face when she bent over and took

Sadey's vitals. "I'm not going to report you because you are a human," she said in a monotone voice.

"O-okay," Sadey said. "That's right. I'm a human." What in heavens was happening right now? Obviously she wasn't a damned human. Her wounds were already healed.

"I think she's fine to release," the man in the corner said. "Don't you, Jody?"

"Release forms," the woman said vacantly. Her pupils were blown out so completely, Sadey couldn't even guess what color her real eyes were. The nurse opened her mouth and froze, lips parted, eyes dead for the span of three breaths before she blinked slowly and said, "You'll need release forms, and then you are free to go. I'll have to take you out in a wheelchair because of hospital policy."

"That won't be necessary," the vamp murmured soothingly.

"That won't be necessary," Jody repeated.

What in the actual hell? Dread blasted through Sadey's veins. He wasn't just a vamp. He was one of the powerful, gifted ones everyone was afraid of, and for good reason. This monster had mind control.

Shit, shit, double shit. Sadey pulled out the IV

someone very determined must've shoved into her arm. They'd wound surgical tape around her arm at least a dozen times to keep her body from rejecting the needle. She had to get out of here.

"I'll get your release forms," Jody said with an empty smile.

Fantastic, but Sadey wasn't signing them. No one here could know her name or Brock would track her down.

The nurse left the room, and now Sadey was terrifyingly alone with the monster in the corner. His navy T-shirt read *Winterset Fire Department* and had the city logo on it. A firefighting vampire? She'd always imagined the undead dressed in tuxedos, drinking goblets of blood in their gothic mansions, not fighting fires and pulling strangers from cars.

"Th-thank you for saving me," she rushed out so perhaps he would remember she was a person and not serial-kill her.

"You smell of fear," he said in a low, gravelly voice, and now his eyes were that pitch black again. He pushed off the wall, stood to his full imposing height, and cocked his head as he studied her. He was the predator, judging whether she was worthy prey.

"If I wanted to hurt you, I wouldn't have covered for you."

Covered for her? "Did you take over that woman's mind?"

His lips stretched into a wide smile, and he whispered, "I'm in all of their heads."

"Are you in mine?" she squeaked out.

That cocky smile faltered, and a troubled expression flashed through his eyes before he carefully composed his expression. "No." His eyes narrowed as he eased back. "For some reason, I don't want to be. I'm Aric."

Oh, he was intoxicating. Surely it was the vamp in him. They were compelling on a chemical level. That's what helped vamps convince their victims to let them drink them up. She had to be careful with him because she would be damned if she was going to be a victim. After Brock, she would rather die than let another man control her.

Out of self-preservation, Sadey refused to give him her name. Slowly, she sat up, but winced when pain zinged up her arm.

"You broke it," Aric said.

"Crap." She stared down at the bruising on her

forearm. Shifter healing was great until it came to broken bones.

"I set it for you before it healed, but it'll be sore for a while."

"How did you know to do that?"

The man's lips lifted in the corners, but he didn't look nice. He looked feral. "Just a hunch. What are you?"

Sadey crossed her arms over her chest and gave the window her attention. It was still full dark outside. Maybe if she ignored him until dawn, he would make like a tree and leaf her the hell alone.

"Bear shifter?"

She cast him a quick glance and stifled the snarl in her throat. "That's none of your business."

"Ah, but that's no fair. You know what I am, right?"

She parted her lips to deny him, but the nurse returned just in time. And good thing because, belatedly, she remembered vamps could sense lies like shifters could. That and the bloodsucker had the unnerving ability to poke around in peoples' minds.

She needed to get away from him, and fast.

Sadey read over the form Jody handed her,

attention carefully angled away from the man who seemed to take up every inch in the small room. *Helgalina Tittywinkles*, she scribbled across the bottom line.

Aric snorted from the corner he'd retreated to, as if he could read what she'd written. Hell, maybe he could.

If she was in her animal form right now, every hair on her back would be standing straight up. In fact, she was surprised her animal was as calm as she was. Usually in the presence of rival predators, she became defensive and wanted to rip out of Sadey's skin. Not now, though. Other than an occasional warning growl when he got too close to their secrets, her animal was curiously content to watch him. Strange. Perhaps her inner beasty didn't realize how much danger she was in.

"Thank you for visiting," Nurse Jody said in that strange, empty voice, and then she stood there, staring at something just over Sadey's head. She went completely still like she was a robot that had just powered down. Geez, this vamp was a trip.

As Sadey sidled past Aric to escape to the door, she whispered, "Will she be okay?"

"Other than some confusion and a little headache later, she'll be fine."

"Great. Bye."

Sadey rubbed her sore arm and made her way down the hallway. One by one, the nurses and doctors she passed came to a stop and froze, eyes staring, pupils blown out. Sadey slowed and looked behind her.

Aric stood there, dark eyebrows drawn down in concentration and something more. Confusion? His mussed hair had fallen down his face on one side as though he'd roughed it up after she'd passed him by.

Sadey looked at all the staff who were frozen like statues in the hallway. How was he not in her mind? How did he choose who to manipulate? And why wasn't she Changing out of fear right now?

Troubled down to her bones, Sadey ripped her gaze away from Aric's and bolted for the door with the glowing green exit sign.

That man was too terrifyingly powerful for his own good, and he was much too interesting for hers.

THREE

What was wrong with him? Aric frowned at the small house with the big front porch.

Sadey. The second her name had brushed his mind when he'd introduced himself, he'd almost retched. He hadn't meant to dip into her mind, and it didn't feel right with her. He didn't give a single fuck about visiting other people's minds if it kept him and his people safe, but tonight he'd gone overboard in an effort to keep a complete stranger's identity protected from the hospital staff.

The breeze kicked up, swaying the elaborate garden she'd planted. Bushes, grasses, and brightly colored flowers were placed tastefully in the front landscaping, down both sides of the house, and around the dogwood tree out front. The grass was mowed, and the landscaping perfectly weeded, the soil damp and smelling of rich earth. Before Sadey had gone inside, cradling her sore arm, she'd talked to each plant as she watered them like they were her children.

This was a woman who reveled in sunlight, so why the fuck couldn't he leave the shadows of this old sycamore tree across the street right now?

For the past ten minutes, he'd tried to convince himself he was just trying to make sure she got home safe. He'd tried to convince himself he was just watching her warily as a predator watches a rival in its territory, but she wasn't a physical danger to him.

Her face had given her away when he'd asked if she was a bear. She was something smaller. She didn't smell like a dragon either, so she wasn't either of the two shifters that could threaten his life and the lives of his coven. Not when she was so obviously alone out here without a crew to protect her.

He didn't like that.

It was dangerous for supes to be alone, and she hadn't even called anyone on the cab ride from the hospital to her house. He'd flown near her taxi in his shifted form and watched for her to lift her phone to her ear, but she didn't. Tonight, she'd almost died, and she had no one to call?

A shallow hiss filled his throat at the idea that her people had failed her so epically.

Movement caught his attention in the front left window. A light had turned on, and now Sadey's shadow walked across the room. She pulled her shirt off gingerly, as though her arm was really hurting.

A reckless thought consumed him. He could dip into her mind briefly and take the pain away. He did that sometimes when he was called to a bad injury on a shift. But the thought of digging around in her mind had him doubled over in pain.

Squatting down in the shadows, Aric glared at her outline. Perfect breasts bobbed out of the bra she removed and, fuck it all, his dick was so hard right now. This wasn't right. He shouldn't be sitting here watching her like this. Why didn't she have blackout curtains? *Because she won't burn to her final death if a ray of sunlight peeks through*, his asshole subconscious whispered.

What was his purpose here? He was fighting something that drew him to her. It rivaled bloodlust, but the thought of drinking her made him feel guilty. This right here was why he made a terrible vampire. His maker, Arabella, had known it would be like this, but she'd Turned him anyway. Wasn't he supposed to be heartless by now? Wasn't he supposed to feel less?

Instead, he felt everything. His coven could sense it and resented him. They thought him weak. If it wasn't for the power of mind-manipulation that had manifested when he'd risen from the dead, they would've put him down by now.

His phone chirped, and he checked the glowing screen. It was Garret, his Second. *Where are you? Dawn is almost here.*

Aric slid his glance to the gray horizon and muttered a curse. This was the part he hated—the fear of the sun.

And for the billionth time since he'd been Turned, he cursed his maker for all she'd taken from him. Arabella had promised him great power, and when he'd turned it down, she'd Turned him anyway. She'd ruined his life with that power.

And now he couldn't have a normal conversation with a woman like Sadey without smelling the stink of fear pouring from her skin.

Aric stood, made his way into the middle of the street, and inhaled deeply. Sadey was a being of the light, and he was of the shadows, and he had no place in her life.

He would be poison to her.

Sadey's shadow froze, and slowly she made her way to the window. He should leave before she saw him and became even more scared, but he couldn't conjure his shift. He just stood there, a dark part of his heart wanting her to see him. Wanting her to know he saw her.

Sadey lifted the thin blinds and then paused, staring at him with those gold eyes that said whatever animal she harbored was close to the surface.

Sexy, mysterious, rogue. He bet her animal was stunning.

But this was enough. It had to be. He had no place being here. Aric closed his eyes and gave his body to the bats.

And then in a haze of smoke, he disappeared into the night and out of her life.

FOUR

Sadey frowned down at the address, then back to the giant Victorian home surrounded by wilderness. It was beautiful, but not at all like the gothic castle she'd imagined a coven of vampires would inhabit. A shallow porch graced the front and was lined with a trio of white rocking chairs to match the intricate railing.

There were a few girls leaning against the railing. They wore sundresses, jean jackets, and cute wedges of differing colors as if they'd called each other and coordinated their outfits. They talked low and laughed easily. Sadey stuck her nose out the open window of her rental car and sniffed. They were definitely human, and they weren't afraid of being at a coven house, so why should she? She was a motherfluffin' shifter. And not just a bird shifter either, but one with teeth and claws. She wasn't defenseless.

Plus, something deep down inside of her said Aric wouldn't hurt her.

She remembered the look on his face right before he'd disappeared in a haze of flocking bats and purple smoke. There had been such a raw vulnerability in his eyes when he'd stood outside her house. That was one week ago, and she hadn't seen hide nor hair of him since. That would've been good except she was curious about him, and apparently that curiosity-killed-the-cat saying didn't work on her. Hopefully the nine lives adage would work, though, because now that she was here, her animal apparently thought this was the greatest idea ever instead of the stupidest.

Sadey huffed a sigh and licked the envelope to the card she'd brought for Aric, then shoved it into her purse. She shoved the door open and jogged across the street.

"Hey, we've got a new girl," one of the human girls said in a friendly tone.

A blonde looked troubled, though. "Who are you here for?"

"Uuuuh." That was a weird question. "Aric?"

The blonde's frown deepened further. "He just fed a couple nights ago, but okay. If he called you in, maybe he had a bad night at work."

"What do you mean?" Sadey asked, a sliver of worry snaking in her gut.

"He's a firefighter, and sometimes his shifts are bad. He has to feed more if he's going to be around all that blood and not hurt the injured ones, you know?"

"Oh. Yes, of course." The silence grew too thick, and she was crap at small talk, so naturally she made it awkward. "So you're all here to feed the vamps?"

The friendly brunette pursed her lips. "Well yeah, the pay doesn't suck. Aren't you?"

Sadey opened her mouth to vehemently deny that she would ever do something so repulsive, but the door opened suddenly, and a tall man with dark hair and green eyes smiled at them and said, "Y'all come on in. Your boys are ready for you."

Sadey's pulse tripped as the man's eyes landed on her and narrowed. "What do we have here? Fresh meat?"

"Garret don't give her a hard time. She's here for Aric," the blonde explained. "The first time is always nerve-wracking, too, so cut her some slack, okay?"

Garret smiled at the blonde and murmured, "So long as you're here for me, darlin'."

The blonde blushed a pretty color, ducked her gaze, and looked pleased as punch. "You know I am."

The girls filed in one by one while Sadey looked longingly behind her at the rental car that sat on the circle drive by the others. Her chariot awaited, but the thought that Aric was right inside, just a few walls away from her, made it impossible to flee. Apparently, her damn animal had grown a keen and terrifying interest in men even more dangerous than Brock. This was the part she hated about being a shifter—the marrow-deep instincts she couldn't ignore.

So like the epic fate-tempter she was, Sadey stepped into the house behind the others. The decorator had been a fan of dark woods. Dark floors, dark wainscoting, dark bronze sconces, and a massive black chandelier hung above her in the entryway. To the left was an entire wall of security panels with video, retinal scanners, and glowing squares of buttons that probably helped make this place a fortress during the day. Made sense. Vampires didn't have much defense when they were sleeping.

Garret led them down a hallway and a set of stairs to a sprawling basement with tall ceilings. Down here, the lights were dimmer, and it smelled of sawdust and new paint, like the coven had recently renovated this place. The brunettes filed off one at a time to bedroom doors and disappeared inside, while Garret draped his arm over Blondie's shoulders.

"You don't have to worry," Blondie said. "It's not scary like rumors say. This coven is gentle and don't even leave scars behind. Aric will treat you well for your work."

Work. Donating blood to vamps was considered a job? Sadey tried to smile, but she was pretty sure it was a grimace highlighted by a lip tremble. Some predator shifter she was.

As Garret opened a bedroom door and waited for Blondie to saunter inside, he tilted his chin to the door at the end of the hallway. "Aric is in there." Garret looked like he wanted to say more, but he frowned at Aric's door instead. And when she hesitated with her hand raised to knock, Garret said,

"Take good care of our king. He shoulders a lot."

King? Holy hell. Royalty was notoriously ruthless. They had to be to secure entire covens under them. She was about to let herself into the king of the coven's room. Crap, oh crap, oh crap.

"Don't worry," Garret said. "Aric will be gentle with you, especially your first time."

Fantastic. Clenching her fists to stifle the instinct to flee the house, she knocked lightly.

There was commotion at the end of the hallway, and when she turned around, the nice brunette was pinned onto the wall, hips rolling against a handsome man with pallid skin and bright blue eyes. They were making out hard core, and from the sounds the brunette was making, she was thoroughly enjoying it. The vamp slid his icy gaze to Sadey right as he opened his mouth and exposed his fangs, then sank them into the brunette's neck. He made a hissing sound as he ground his hips against her.

Oh my gosh, oh my gosh!

The door swung open, and Aric froze like an ice sculpture. His face went slack, and his gray eyes morphed to the black of a raven's feather. He wore nothing but low-slung jeans. She'd known he was well-built through his firefighter shirt, but he was more cut than she'd even imagined. The dim lighting made deep shadows between his hard pecs and between each hard ridge of his six-pack. The tattoos she'd seen peeking out of his shirt were dark against his pallid skin. He was intimidatingly sexy.

With a rapid blink, Aric looked at the sexual feeding frenzy down the hall and yanked Sadey by the arm inside of his room.

The door clicked closed, and he was there, standing too close, his hand digging into her arm too hard. "What the hell are you doing here?" he whispered. "I'm not drinking you!"

"I'm not here for that," she gritted out. "I came to give you something."

Aric ran his hand through his chestnut brown hair, mussing it as he looked around with a tinge of panic flaring in his eyes. It was then that she really saw his bedroom. It was massive, but okay, that made sense. He was king of this coven after all.

It was dark, with just a few sconces lit on the walls. Rich wood floors and chocolate-colored walls made the room seem even darker.

"It's like a classy dungeon in here," she said with a

nervous laugh. “Where’s the shackles?”

He gave her a disapproving look, so she muttered, “Joke,” and moved to the writing desk scattered with charcoal sketches. Some were of animals, some of planes or scenery. Each was dark and smudged quickly, but belied real skill. Under a picture of a row of familiar flowers, there was an eye done in such detail she gasped. Gently, she moved the image of landscaping over and exposed a picture of a girl lying in a man’s arms, her lips parted slightly, her eyes wide and wild, a tear streaking through the dark smudges on her face. If this was done in color, those eyes would be gold.

“This is me,” she uttered, shocked.

“You shouldn’t be here, Sadey.”

“How do you know my name?” she asked, rounding on him.

“It’s not safe. If my coven finds out what you are—”

“How do you know my name, Aric?”

His chin was dipped to his chest, but Aric lifted his dark gaze to hers. “It was an accident. I saw the name. You were loud.”

“What do you mean?”

"When I told you my name in the hospital, you said yours back. In your head."

"You said you weren't in my head." She retreated a couple of steps until her back hit the sketching table. She felt violated. "You lied."

"I didn't lie. I didn't. I don't want to be in your mind. It feels..." He shook his head hard. "It makes me feel sick. It's not something I had control over, though. You were reaching for me. You're reaching for me now. Begging me to..."

"Begging you to what?"

"Apologize."

"Fuck," she gritted out. "This was a mistake. I've done this before. I've been with someone who wanted every piece of me, and I'm not doing this again."

"Why are you here?"

"I can't." Sadey strode for the door, but Aric pulled her arm, and now his eyes were roiling like black flames.

"Why?" he gritted out. "I want to know because I've been doing my part. I've been staying away from you, but now you're in my bedroom, and I can hear you in my head. I can feel you."

Sadey couldn't catch her breath. Not here where he was leveling her insides with that impassioned look. Not when he was touching her. Not as his grip lessened, not when his thumb brushed the inside of her arm so softly it made her body react.

"Do you drink girls like the ones outside?" she asked. The answer mattered so much.

"Yes."

Her heart fell, and she sighed out her disappointment.

"It isn't sexual for me," he said.

"How can I believe that after what I saw in the hall? That woman was enjoying it—"

"Listen to my voice, Sadey." Aric gently pulled her closer, and now both of his hands were on her arms. "You can hear a lie. It's not sexual for me. I have to eat, that's all."

Truth. But... "How can I trust what you say when you can manipulate my mind?"

"I wouldn't with you." He cupped her neck with those cold, strong hands of his and raised his dark brows, leveled her with the honesty in his eyes, and repeated in a whisper, "I wouldn't."

And she believed him. She had to. Her animal did.

"I won't hurt you, but you can't leave right now. Not this soon after coming in. My coven will think something is wrong. Please, just stay for a little while."

Her gaze flicked to the unmade four poster bed across the room before she could stop herself. Aric frowned and looked behind him, following her gaze.

"Why did you draw me?" she asked on a breath. "Why did you draw my landscaping? Why were you standing outside of my house that night?"

"Because," he murmured.

"Tell me why or I'm leaving, and screw the consequences."

"Dammit, Sadey, I'm trying to protect you."

"Why?"

"Because I feel compelled to! Because it feels like this world would be uglier without you here. Because you make me feel things I haven't felt in a really long time. Things I thought I wasn't capable of anymore."

Before she could stop herself, Sadey lifted up on her tiptoes and pressed her lips to his. It was reckless and wrong, but his words stirred something wild within her. She knew exactly what he meant. She made him feel. She understood. She thought she'd hate men until the day she died after the hell Brock had put her through, but here she was, feeling alive again. And it had been so damn long. Aric couldn't be more wrong for her. He had a life leading a dangerous coven of vampires. He bled people, fed on them. He was a creature of the night and completely incapable of giving her a relationship she needed. But he could give her something she wanted—an escape. An hour where she didn't feel jaded and unlovable. He was dangerous, powerful, and sexy, and she wanted him to touch her body, her soul, and yes, maybe her mind was reaching for him because she wanted someone to touch her there, too.

Aric had gone still with her kiss, but then his hand went around the back of her head. He angled his face, dipped closer, and then pushed his tongue past her lips. Sadey shuddered with how good he felt touching her. She ran her hand down his chest to his abs and reveled in the feeling of his taut muscles twitching under her touch.

Aric lifted her off the ground with a wild sound in his throat and slammed her back against the door. His kiss became desperate as he pressed his rock-hard erection between her thighs. When she wrapped her legs around his waist, his hand was there, strong on the back of her knee, encouraging her to stay just like this, curved around his body. Sadey hugged his neck and moaned as he dipped his tongue into her mouth over and over, rocking his hips smoothly, hitting her clit just right.

She was burning up, and this was all too fast, but for the life of her, she couldn't conjure a single care. She couldn't stop this right now if she tried. Aric yanked her away from the door and walked her slowly back toward the bed.

Sadey lowered her lips to his neck and sucked hard, and the hiss in his throat revved her up even hotter. His hands were strong on her, as if he knew what her body was capable of. He didn't need to be gentle because she wasn't some fragile human. She had an animal side that reveled in rough affection. Teasingly, she clamped her teeth on his neck. Silly vamp, offering a predator his throat. He must trust her.

Aric held her tighter and eased them onto the bed, ground his erection against her. His skin was so cold on hers. As he leaned down and took her mouth, he slid his hands up inside of her shirt, brushed her ribs, and cupped her breast. Damn bra. Desperate to touch more of his skin, she pulled off her shirt. Aric eased up just enough to let the fabric slip between them, and then his lips crashed onto hers again.

His hands were rough in her hair, and she fucking loved it. Loved the way he angled her face back to level her lips with biting kisses. Loved how he trailed his kisses along her jaw to her neck, hesitated there to suck on her skin, then moved down. He undid the clasp of her bra and yanked it off, then sucked on her nipple until she arched against the mattress. She spread her legs for him, inviting him closer.

Reaching down, she popped the button of his jeans and unzipped them so he wouldn't be confused by mixed signals.

"Tell me to stop now, Sadey," he growled out.

"I don't want you to stop," she said breathily.

"Fuck," he muttered, and then her pants were on the floor with his. Just a second was all he had needed to unfasten them and strip them off her legs.

He ground his hips again, and she could feel the head of his swollen shaft at her wet entrance, and a sudden desperation took her. "Please," she whispered, digging her nails into his back.

His lips were on her neck again, and there were the sharp points of his fangs, but he wouldn't drink her. Not if she didn't tell him to. She didn't know how she knew, but she did. She could trust Aric not to hurt her.

When he eased back, there was raw hunger in his eyes. It should've terrified her, but it didn't. Instead, the heat in her stomach turned molten. How sexy to be wanted so desperately by someone. Fuck Brock and his memory. Fuck her ex for forcing her to pick up the scraps of his affection. Fuck his other mates. Right here, right now, she was enough for Aric.

"You're more than enough," he whispered, pushing into her. "Don't reach, Sadey. I can't keep out if you reach for me."

But keeping him out seemed like a lot of work when she could barely think straight. Aric pushed into her again, stretching her, filling her. She gasped out a helpless sound as his lips collided with hers. His abs flexed against her with every stroke he pumped into her. His smooth, cold skin stole the warmth from hers. His sharp teeth grazed her lips and still, he felt perfect right now. So perfect.

"You're the perfect one," he murmured against

her lips. Gritting his teeth, he moaned and bucked into her again, gripped her waist. "Fuck, you feel so good."

The pressure built to blinding in her middle. How could anything feel like this? How could she feel this connected with another person? His lips were back on her throat, his teeth right there, and his look of hunger from before flashed through her mind. Her stomach turned with a sudden desperation for something to sate her thirst. What was he doing to her?

He slid into her again, so hard, so good, and she lost her mind completely to the release she teetered right on the edge of. "Do it."

"Do what?" he ground out.

"Drink me."

There was no hesitation. His teeth pierced her throat, and it should've hurt, but it didn't. Not when her orgasm exploded through her body at that exact moment. "*It's okay. Okay, okay. It's okay.*" The words tumbled around in her mind, echoing, tripping over each other. "*I'll take care of you.*" Aric was there in her head making beautiful promises.

God, what an alluring offer. She hadn't been taken

care of in a really long time.

His hand gripped the side of her neck as he rammed into her and froze, his shaft pulsing as the first jet of heat shot into her. He sucked on her neck hard, bit deeper, and she groaned with how incredible her body felt. He pushed into her again and again, drawing every aftershock from her as he emptied himself completely. And as the final, faint pulse of her release subsided, Aric loosened his jaw, released her torn neck, and licked where he'd bitten her.

Her skin sealed with her shifter healing, and he sucked gently there as if he was silently thanking her.

He hadn't taken much from her. Not even enough to make her feel faint or for her fingertips to turn cold. He'd stayed in control and only sipped at her through their orgasm. It shouldn't have been, but that was the sexiest thing she'd ever been a part of. What did that say about her? Right now, she didn't care. Not when Aric was trailing kisses down her collar bone and stroking along her arm, coveting her. And she repaid him in kind—kissing his skin, biting him gently, rubbing her cheek against his affectionately. She would never tell him, but that was a sign of deep adoration for shifters like her.

Aric lifted up and smiled as though he'd heard that last thought. And then slowly, he eased forward and nuzzled his cheek against hers. Her chest heated with something unexplainable. Something incredible, blinding, and overwhelming.

The door creaked open. "Hey boss, do you have any extra twenties?" Garret asked. "Oh, shit!"

With a gasp, Sadey covered her face in mortification as Aric threw the covers over them. "Garret, get out!"

Sadey peeked through her fingers, but Garret was standing there, staring at Aric with such a strange frown on his face. "What's happening right now?"

"Garret, I'm serious, get the fuck out of my room. That's an order."

Garret's eyes narrowed to slits as he dragged an angry gaze to Sadey. "What did you do to him?"

Aric blasted off her, melded into a thick plume of bats and smoke and waved violently this way and that until there was a deafening crash. Aric was across the room and pinning Garret to the wall, which had shattered behind him. "I gave you an order, so why the fuck are you still here? How I feed is my business."

"Except that wasn't just feeding!" Garret yelled. "I can feel your goddamned bond."

He lifted an accusatory gaze to Sadey, but she was crouched defensively on the bed, ready to Change and rip his throat out if the vamp came a step closer.

Garret huffed a humorless breath. "All right, *King*. I'm leaving." He lifted his hands in surrender as power hummed through the room.

When Aric pushed off Garret, he was holding a splintered piece of two-by-four against Garret's chest, right over his heart.

Garret meandered to the door but paused at the open doorframe. "Nice eyes, shifter," he growled out with one last hate-filled glance at Sadey.

The slamming door rattled the room, and Aric yelled a feral sound and chucked the two-by-four against the wall so hard it speared the sheetrock and hung there, five feet above the ground, shaking from the force.

And she could feel it now, too. Something invisible tethered them and drew taut as he paced away, then eased when he came closer again.

Hand over the hot spot on her chest, she asked,

"What just happened?"

Aric settled his hands on his hips and shook his head over and over. And when he lifted those pitch-colored, blazing eyes to her, she could see it there—the realization of what they'd just done.

"I didn't just feed on you, Sadey. I think I gave you a claiming mark."

FIVE

Aric wanted to break everything after that meeting with his coven. Such vitriol had spewed forth from his people, he wanted to throttle every last one of them.

His truck nearly went up on two wheels as he turned into Sadey's driveway, but when he slammed on his brakes and rocked to a stop, he couldn't understand the scene before him.

Her rental car had all its doors wide open, and the trunk was packed with boxes. The *ding, ding* of the keys in the ignition sounded, and the front door to her house was wide open. One of the boxes had tipped over, and the porch was scattered with papers and books. Long claw marks ran down the side of the box.

What in the hell?

Slowly, Aric slid out from his ride and froze, listening for Sadey. He took the keys from the ignition to stop the annoying sound. They jingled in his hand as he made his way across the yard to the porch stairs. The floorboards creaked under his shoes as he peeked inside her house. Boxes were everywhere, but that made no damn sense—she'd only left his house two hours ago. That wasn't enough time to do this amount of packing.

He locked his arms against the doorframe, his frown so deep his forehead ached. "Sadey?" he called out carefully.

Nothing. No scuffle of her shoes, no clatter of rushed packing, no greeting. He listened harder, but there was nobody here. There was no pulse in the house. "Shhhit," he murmured, pushing off the door. He couldn't go in without her invite, but he didn't need to. Sadey was in the wind.

Aric rested his hands on his hips and glared down at the shredded box thoughtfully. He inhaled deeply. Fur and Sadey. And that's when he felt it—the hair raising on the back of his neck that said he was being watched. That he was being hunted.

He scanned the woods around the house, but even with his heightened night vision, he couldn't see the reflective eyes that would tell him his hunch was right. Clever little predator.

Inhaling deeply, he hopped over the last couple of stairs on the porch and made his way slowly to the tree line. His scorched arm tingled, as if reminding him what had happened the last time he'd messed with a pissed-off shifter, but that was different. Sadey was different, and he couldn't even imagine what she was going through right now. Anger, maybe, but definitely fear over what they'd done. She had grabbed her purse and left his house, him trailing after her, begging her to stay and talk about the claiming mark. And that's when he'd seen a name in her mind—Brock. She'd thought that name with such hatred he'd almost missed the fear she kept bundled in the middle of all that anger.

She'd been hurt, and now look what Aric had done. He'd linked her to him—a complete stranger. He'd given himself power over her. The thought of it made him want to double over with the ache in his chest. This wasn't how it was supposed to happen. He was supposed to choose a human woman who could make him forget his maker. The law said registered vampires could Turn one human, one mate, one forever-love. And what had he done? He'd chosen a shifter, who couldn't be Turned and who didn't want the bond.

He deserved her claws.

Maple and birch trees towered over him, and as the blue moonlight filtered through the sparse branches, it created a spiderweb of shadows on the forest floor. It would be spring soon, but right now, the wind was bitterly cold. When he'd been human, he'd loved nights like this. Big moon, chilly-wind nights where he would sit near a fire pit in his old backyard, drink beer and shoot the shit with his friends from his old life. Now his friends were all vampires, and beer tasted like soggy ashes. Sadey had been a beautiful distraction from his anger over his new life, and now he'd hurt her.

When he stepped on a twig, it snapped loudly. Freezing into place, one leg locked against the soft ground, one leg bent and resting on the toe of his boot, he listened for a heartbeat. That was one advantage to his job. He could hear the pulse tripping, fading, or holding strong. He could listen to the *thud, thud* of a victim's heart and know how much time he had to work on them. But here in Sadey's dark woods, he couldn't hear a thin—

Bam!

Aric fell forward under a great weight, as if he'd been shot in the back by a cannon. He hit the ground hard and resisted the urge to shift and give the bats his body to escape the pain. Sadey snarled as he rolled over and covered his face from her raking claws. Desperate to see her, he opened his eyes, and his breath clogged his throat.

She was beautiful and not at all what he'd expected. Why? Because shifters like Sadey didn't exist.

Pain slashed across his neck, and then she was at him, teeth on his throat, dragging him backward.

"Sadey, I'm sorry!" he gasped out.

The massive snow leopard stopped, every muscle still. She loosened her powerful jaws and dropped him. Aric was bleeding and clawed up, but it was nothing his swift healing wouldn't fix. Right now, the important thing was that she had taken a few steps back and was looking at him uncertainly. The snarl was softer in her throat, and when he moved to sit up, she lowered to her belly and hissed out a warning.

Aric held out his hands in surrender. "I'm so sorry. I didn't even think about my bite bonding us. It's never bonded me to anyone before."

Sadey pulled her lips back over her long, curved canines and hissed louder.

Right, don't mention the other girls. He was definitely going to screw this up. He'd sucked at relationships when he was human, and his maker had broken him the rest of the way. "Look, I should've thought it through. I forgot about shifters and claiming marks, but I should've remembered. I should've stopped us. I tried to stop us!"

Sadey eased up on all fours, her ears flattened back, her muzzle wrinkled up in a snarl. She was stunning. Her thick silver coat was speckled with dark spots. Curved, razor-sharp claws extended from her massive paws and dug into the soil. Her swishing tail was long and thicker than any of the other big cat shifters. It was so strange to see the same light gold eyes he hadn't been able to get out of his mind on a snow leopard.

Aric had a million questions. How had she come to be? This animal didn't exist in shifters, yet here she was staring uncertainly at him. He wanted to know every single thing about the mysterious woman who was wrecking the cement walls he'd built around his heart.

Aric sat on his folded legs, hands out, palms up. He was no threat to her. Even though he was stronger, more powerful, even though he had more weapons than she did, he couldn't defend himself if it meant hurting her. "I tried to stay away from you," he whispered. "I'm so sorry."

Sadey blinked hard, then shook her head. She stared off into the woods. Such a heartbroken sound rattled from her chest. She bunched her muscles as if she would bolt, but instead she sauntered over to him and ran her giant head under his arm, curved her body around his back, and rubbed up his other side. Her snarl changed. It softened. And as Aric carefully ran his hand over her head, it began to sound more like a purr than a growl. She lay across his lap and rolled, swatting him lightly with her paw. One of her claws hooked into the fabric of his T-shirt, but she didn't move to rip it. She just lay there, looking up at him with those blazing eyes of hers, one side of her mouth curled up in a playful expression as her purr rattled on.

He chuckled and lifted her giant paw to his face, pressed the pink pads against his jaw. With a sigh, he murmured, "Can you Change back yet?"

Now both sides of her mouth curled back, and she let off another unhappy hiss. But after a few seconds, she pushed off him and sauntered back the way he'd come. And when she was past the branch he'd stepped on, she paused and looked at him over her shoulder, her thick tail twitching. The fury had faded from her eyes, and now she seemed to be asking him, "What are you waiting for?"

Aric couldn't help the smile that stretched his face as he rocked upward. He probably looked like shit—bleeding, tattered clothes, neck clawed to hell, but he didn't care about any of that now. All he cared about was Sadey, waiting up ahead for him. When he stepped into line with her, he brushed his fingertips down her back, and she moved off again, content to walk beside him back to her house.

And this was the moment. This was the instant that an old, almost-forgotten feeling unfurled in his chest. Everything had been so heavy since he'd been Turned, but out here in Sadey's woods, a familiar sensation came over him. For a few seconds, he couldn't put a name to it, but when she looked up at him, filling the night woods with the thick rattle of her content purr, it struck him.

For the first time in a really long time, he felt hope.

SIX

Sadey pulled the long-sleeved sleep shirt over her head in a rush, and then padded into the living room. She sidled around a stack of boxes that stretched up to the ceiling and shoved her feet into a pair of snow boots that had toppled over beside the door. She moved to leave, but on second thought grabbed the card out of her purse before she stepped outside.

Aric was on the front porch, shoving all the papers back into the box she'd shredded after her accidental Change.

She cleared her throat nervously. "It's been a long time since I Changed unexpectedly like that. I usually have a lot more control."

"It's okay. I wanted to lose my shit after you left,

too."

Aric seemed like the quiet type who could go from zero to terrifying vamp in seconds. He also seemed like a man who kept himself in tight control.

"Why didn't you?"

"Because Garret called a meeting and told my people what happened."

"Right, because you're King of the Winterset Coven."

Aric huffed a breath and ran his hands through his hair. His eyes were the soft gray of a dove's breast right now, and much less intimidating than the pitch black they turned when he was riled up. "I'm actually the King of the Asheville Coven. Or…" He frowned. "I was."

"Are you not staying in Winterset?"

He looked around pointedly at the boxes strewn about. "Are you?"

Oh, he was an evasive, sexy vamp. Fine, if he wanted to answer questions with questions, she would play his game. "What happened at your meeting?"

He shook his head for a long time, gave his attention to the woods beside her house.

"Your coven doesn't like me much, do they?" she asked.

With an irritated sigh, Aric sat down on the old porch swing and draped his arm over the back, kicked it into a gentle rocking motion with the heel of his boot and stared at her until she gave in and sat beside him. And then he explained. "Choosing you would've been different six months ago."

"How so?"

The creaking of the swing was the only noise for a while, and it occurred to her that Aric was very careful with choosing his words. Maybe he had to be because he was a king, she didn't know.

"I was barely able to avoid a war with the shifters."

"Which shifters?"

"All of them."

Sadey's eyeballs nearly bugged out of her head. "What happened?"

"My maker, Arabella, was very old and undergoing The Sickening. She was the queen of my coven, losing her mind slowly, and she became cruel. She stalked a shifter—a grizzly. And she badgered and bribed him until he agreed to be her consort."

"Consort?" Why did that word taste like poison on her tongue?

"Yeah. She fed from him when she wanted and paid him a lot of money. She wanted someone else to hurt. Someone strong who would heal and who could withstand more pain. She wanted something to feed on that wouldn't die easily. She wanted something to scar on the outside and the inside."

"Oh, my gosh," Sadey murmured, feeling nauseous.

"Eventually, the bear tired of being her plaything and rebelled. And on the night Arabella planned to torture him back into submission, his crew began arriving."

"Who was his crew?"

"The Bloodrunners."

She bolted upright on the swing. "Holy. Shit."

"You know of them?"

"Yeah, everyone does. Female fire-breathing dragon shifter as alpha, two grizzlies, and two birds of prey with some of the most dominant lineages in the world running through their veins."

"That would be them. Only Arabella couldn't let go of torturing the bear, so she went after the dragon-blooded alpha as revenge and dragged our entire coven along with her for that shit-tastic idea."

"What happened?"

"Uuuh." Aric rocked his head backward and rolled his eyes closed. "Arabella, my queen, my maker, was killed. And as her Second, I took the coven and was supposed to avenge her death. I had to appease my coven and keep us from war with the Bloodrunners because it would've escalated. It wouldn't just be the Asheville Coven against the Bloodrunners. The crew threatened to bring in every crew of shifters from every country. Vampires number at two-hundred in the world. We would've put up one hell of a fight, but we don't have the numbers for a war like that. I had to walk a really fine line and make some really hard decisions to save my people."

"So that's why your coven isn't on board with…us."

Aric brushed his fingertips against her arm. She had gooseflesh from a combination of the cold and his horrifying story about the Bloodrunners. In a blur, he pulled the blanket off the back of the swing and settled it over her legs.

"They aren't big shifter fans right now, no," he

murmured. "Hell, they aren't a big fan of me, and I'm their king. The things I had to do... It's too soon for them to completely trust me again, and now I've bonded to someone they see as a threat."

"Well, they won't have to worry about me," she murmured, her voice shaking with emotion. God, just the thought of leaving him now made her chest feel like it was caving in. "I came to your house tonight to say goodbye. And to give you this." She handed him the card.

Aric searched her eyes for the span of a few breaths before he gently took the crimson red envelope from her hand. He took his time ripping into the flap, then pulled the handmade card out slowly. On the front, she'd drawn a cartoon smiling vampire with a fireman's hat and a hose in his hand. Aric huffed an amused sound, then opened it up. "You don't suck," he read out loud. "Thanks for saving me." His voice cracked on the last word, and he swallowed hard before he closed up the card and put it back inside the envelope. "Why are you leaving?"

Sadey sighed and relaxed against his side, drew her knees up under the blanket. "It's a long story."

Aric stared out over the yard at the dark horizon.

"I have about four hours until dawn. I have time for a long story."

But sharing her secrets was a terrifying thought. It was something she hadn't shared with anyone. Too much shame, too much fear. Too much vulnerability that would allow the man who was stealing her heart to really *see* her. She wanted to keep his good opinion of her. "I just can't stay longer than I already have."

"Because of Brock?"

"How do you know that name?"

"You reached."

Shit. A growl vibrated up her throat before she could stop it, but hang it all, she didn't want to do this. She'd wanted to start over and move on, not dredge up a past she hated. But Aric was bonded to her now, and even if they were about to be separated, he should know something real about her. "When I was in that wreck last week, I didn't just lose control of the wheel like I told the police. I was forced off the road by an old black Chevy pickup truck."

"What?" Aric snarled out, and when Sadey looked up, his face had turned terrifying, his eyes as dark as night.

The hairs rose all over her body as power, anger,

and dominance pressed against her.

"I never saw the driver's face, and I didn't recognize the truck. I tried to convince myself it was just a drunk driver, or someone texting who got too afraid to stop and check on me. I tried to convince myself it had nothing to do with Brock because I wanted so badly to stay here. I like Winterset. I'm happy here. I feel settled for the first time maybe ever. And then there was you, and I couldn't stop thinking about you. I couldn't stop wondering why you worked so hard to save me and then covered for me at the hospital. I couldn't get your face out of my head. I even had a dream about you." A dirty one with lots of pelvic thrusting that woke her up in a cold sweat, but Aric didn't have to know that part. *Don't reach!* "As much as I want to ignore my instincts, something keeps nagging at me that it wasn't an accident. That the person behind the wheel was sent here to hurt me."

"Why would Brock send someone to run you off the road?" Aric asked carefully. He wasn't fooling her, though. His voice was too deep, and his last word tapered off into a terrifying hiss.

"I'm not supposed to exist. The snow leopard

wasn't a shifter animal until a few generations ago when one popped up randomly. The first was born to a couple of ordinary leopard shifters. Somehow, three other snow leopards were born the next generation, none of them connected by blood, and all to big cat shifter couples. I linked up with a crew of snow leopards all around my same age because it felt like the safe thing to do. Other than myself, there were two females and one male. Brock was my alpha."

"Was he your mate?"

"He said he was all of our mates. The other girls were fine with the crew how it was. The manipulation happened slowly, so I didn't even notice how controlling Brock was until I was in deep. There were no bonds, no claiming marks, nothing like that. But I cared for my crew because I wasn't alone, you know? None of our parents had registered us because you know how it is with the rare shifters. They're stalked, recruited, studied...killed. We aren't like the bears. We don't have the numbers to defend ourselves." Aric would understand. He'd had to protect his people too. "Brock decided we would be like the gorilla shifters and have multiple mates so we could boost our numbers. It became about procreation and furthering our species. Anna and Violet ate it up. They just...thrived under the attention they could secure from Brock. Violet got pregnant right away, and she was coveted, and Anna got pregnant six months later. But I wasn't happy, and the idea of being bound to Brock by a child dropped me into a dark place. I wanted more. I wanted someone to love me. I wanted to raise cubs with a man I thought would be a good father for them. I wanted to be someone's everything, but Brock could barely look at me when we were together. I was at the bottom of the crew, the least important. I was only there because of my animal. I annoyed the others, and they picked on me, Brock especially. And after Violet and Anna's cubs were born, I was just there as a caretaker for the babies. I told Brock I wanted more out of my life, and that night was the first and only time he hit me. He just...*blasted* his fist across my jaw. Broke it. He told me if I ever left his crew, he wouldn't stop until I was dead because I *belonged* to him. And I believed him. I just knew down to my marrow he would end my life if I left. But then, wasn't I already dead? I'd let a man put his hands on me. I'd let a man convince me I was worthless. I'd slipped into a life I hated, and I knew if I didn't run then, I never would, and I would live out the rest of my days in complete darkness."

Aric wouldn't meet her eyes anymore, though his arm stayed tight around her shoulders. "How long ago did you leave him?"

"Six months. I literally closed my eyes and put my finger on a map, landed on Winterset, packed a few bags, and then left in the night. Six months here, and I feel like I'm finding the things I used to love about myself. I feel more myself, but I'm always looking over my shoulder, waiting for him to show up. Waiting for him to take everything away."

"He won't."

"But you don't know that."

"I do, Sadey," Aric said, leveling her with those demon-black eyes of his. "I won't let him hurt you ever. I don't want you to run anymore."

"What are you saying?"

"I'm saying stay. Stay and set up your life here. Stay and go out with me and—"

"Aric, we're strangers."

"Bullshit. I had to force myself not to come back here night after night because you felt big. I know you're scared. I know it must be terrifying to go through what you did with that domineering asshole and then be bound to a man you don't know. I get it. I'm scared, too, but from the second you opened your eyes out by that wreck, you felt important. You felt like you would make things easier, better."

"Make what easier?"

"Arabella was my Brock. I fell for her before I knew what she was, and when I found out she was a vampire, I tried to break it off. I had this incredible life. Friends, family. I had a great job at a fire station I loved. My life was all lake trips on the weekends, four-wheeling, rock-climbing, camping trips with my friends. I was happy, and she Turned me anyway."

"Against your will?"

His jaw clenched so hard a muscle jumped there. "I loved the sunlight. I loved my life, and she stole everything from me. I know about wanting to leave. I know about the anger. You were braver than me, Sadey. Stronger. You left the bad behind, while I became the king of my coven."

And now she could see him. Really see him. He wasn't one of the heartless vampires she'd been taught to fear. He had been broken like her but had dug in his heels. He thought she was the strong one, the brave one, but he was the one who took over his coven and cared for his people enough to keep them from war. To keep them from complete annihilation. He cared enough to facilitate change in them. To curb their violent tendencies and bring them around to a softer way of thinking. He'd kept his old job of saving people because he cared in a way that was unnatural for the creature of the dark Arabella had turned him into.

His coven probably didn't realize it, but Aric was likely the best thing that had ever happened to them.

And now Garret's murmured words when she'd knocked on Aric's bedroom door made perfect sense. *Take good care of our king. He shoulders a lot.*

Aric was possibly the strongest and most admirable man she'd ever known.

No wonder her animal had chosen him.

No wonder she'd allowed Aric's bite to bond them.

"I like when you make that sound," he murmured, locking her in his gaze. His eyes had lightened to a dawn gray now. "I like when you're happy."

She giggled as her cheeks heated with a blush. "I

didn't realize I was purring."

The slight smile dipped from his lips when he dropped his gaze to her mouth. Slowly, he leaned down and sipped at her lips. With a helpless noise, Sadey melted into him and slipped her arms around his taut waist. He brushed his tongue against the closed seam of her lips in silent question, and she opened for him. He dragged her closer as he dipped his tongue to hers, and she rested her fingertips on his chiseled jaw just to feel the muscles work there.

This wasn't the passionate, fire-catching kisses he'd given her earlier. This one convinced her that perhaps this growing bond between them wasn't a mistake. That maybe it was Fate's way of making up for Brock's shortcomings. Maybe she'd needed to go through that awful ordeal with him to fully appreciate when a good man came into her life.

Heaviness evaporated from her shoulders as he held her. It disappeared completely when he brushed his finger down her cheek and rested his touch onto her neck, right where he'd bitten her. Slowly, he pulled her into his lap until she straddled him. Sadey thought he would push for more because she could feel his thick erection pressed between her legs. But he didn't. Instead, he gave her three, sweet, smacking kisses, then secured the blanket around her shoulders and relaxed back, pulling her with him. And he hugged her. Just rested his chin against her shoulder and held her in a way that cinched up some of her shattered pieces.

Her eyes burned with emotion, but she blinked hard so she wouldn't cry here with Aric. These tears were left over from Brock, and they didn't belong here now.

He rubbed her back in gentle circles and whispered, "Please stay."

And suddenly she wanted to. She wanted to be strong and brave like Aric. She wanted to dig her heels into a place and make it hers. She wanted to stop living a half-life on the run. She wanted to see this thing through with the man who had saved her life, covered for her, thought of her, and drew her face. She wanted to see if there was a life with the good man her animal had chosen.

"Okay," she murmured.

"Okay what?"

Oh, he wanted her to say it out loud so he had no doubts. So he could hear the honesty in her voice, and she got it. If he was the one thinking of leaving, she would want that same security, too.

Sadey inhaled his clean, crisp scent and nuzzled his neck affectionately, then smiled against his skin. “Okay, Aric. I’ll stay.”

SEVEN

Sadey leaned against her rental car outside the firehouse, waiting for the clock to hit five a.m. Aric's boss, Fire Chief Lang, always let him off in plenty of time to get home before dawn if they weren't out on a call, and since the fire truck was still parked in the towering garage, the excitement in her middle had been growing for the past half hour.

The nights he was on shift were the hardest because she didn't get to see him much that day. The past week had been amazing. Every minute spent with him made her feel more alive, more vibrant. So it wasn't a normal dating relationship. They couldn't go out during the day, but she'd always been a night owl anyway, and her online graphic design job allowed her to work odd hours that she could move around to get more time with the man she was falling in love with.

She would much rather deal with the oddities of this relationships than the abusive one with Brock.

Aric was teaching her she could trust people again. He was showing her there was still good people in the world, and he was the best she'd ever met. He was easy with his compliments, and an easy smiler. He was sensitive when she'd had a rough day, and she could tell he tried to tamp his brutal vampire instincts around her.

One thing that hadn't happened, though? Aric had taken her out on dates, talked for hours and hours on her front porch, but past kissing and petting, he had been avoiding intimacy.

That shit ended now.

A happy purr crawled up the back of her throat. She was on the hunt because he'd been revving her up for days with his gentle touches and how damn sexy he looked. Even his laugh melted her into a puddle of hormones.

Aric waved to someone in the garage she couldn't see from this angle, then he shouldered a gear bag and strode a few steps out of the station. His nostrils flared slightly, and he jerked his attention to her. Despite his greeting smile, his eyes were too dark, too hungry.

Maybe it had been a rough shift.

"Hey," he said in that deep, sexy timbre of his as he jogged across the street. He slipped his hands to her waist and pulled her close. "This is a good surprise."

"I didn't want to wait for you to come tell me good night. Or…good morning? I wanted to spend extra minutes with you."

Aric chuckled and lifted her knuckles to his lips, let them linger there before he said, "You missed me."

She giggled and play-nipped his chest. "I always miss you."

"Who are you?" a man called from the open door of the firehouse garage. A taller man in a fire department T-shirt jogged over and stood beside the other, who was squinting into the dark at her.

Aric nodded his head toward them and pulled her hand, led her back to the station. His eyes might be dark and roiling with something she didn't understand, but Aric's steps were light and confident as he pulled her in front of him and rested his hands on top of her shoulders. "John, Nick, this is Sadey. She's my…" Aric cleared his throat and frowned at them each in turn. "She's mine."

The taller one, Nick, jacked up his dark eyebrows. "Whoa, vamp has a girlfriend."

But that didn't sound right. He was more to her, and from the way Aric acted, she was more to him as well.

Beside her, Aric was as tense as a stretched rubber band, and his eyes were narrowed suspiciously on his fellow firefighters like he expected them to stake him at any moment.

He'd told her about the tension in the crew already. They were supposed to be close-knit, because their lives often depended on each other when they were out on calls, but Aric was struggling to adjust to the new station.

Sadey shook their hands and politely murmured, "Nice to meet you. Aric has told me a lot about you."

"Oh, yeah?" John asked. "Anything good?"

"Hell no," Aric muttered. But his tone was softer, teasing maybe, and when she looked up at him, he wore a slight smile just at the corners of his lips.

Sadey giggled and played along. "It's true. He goes on and on about what assholes you both are."

"My feelings are hurt," Nick said with a grin at Aric.

"I'm pretty sure it's impossible to hurt your feelings," Aric murmured. He intertwined his fingers in Sadey's. "Night." Aric led Sadey to her ride, but behind them Nick called out, "Bye, Sadey!" in a baiting tone.

John was making kissing sounds and poked a finger rhythmically into the hole he'd made with the other hand.

Sadey laughed. She couldn't help it. "Y'all stay out of trouble."

"*You* stay out of trouble, Sadey!" John called. "Protect your neck from Blood-Suck Aric!"

She was snickering like a lunatic as she climbed into the passenger's seat. Aric was holding the door open for her, but he had a troubled furrow between his dark brows.

"What's wrong?" she asked as he climbed in behind the wheel.

He turned the engine and pulled out onto the two lane road. "I wouldn't bite you without permission."

"I know that."

He ran his hands over his clean-shaven jaw and took a left, headed back to her house. And it struck her. His dark eyes, the gaunt look of his face. "How long has it been since you fed?"

"It doesn't matter."

"It does to me. How long?"

Aric clenched his jaw once before he leaned back in the seat and draped one arm over the steering wheel. "Since you."

"Aric," she drawled out in admonishment. "It's been a week!"

"Well it hasn't felt right calling one of the girls after bonding with you. Everything has been perfect." He flashed her a dark-eyed glance, then dragged his gaze back to the road. "I know you don't like the idea of me drinking the other girls, and I don't want to rock the boat when you make me this fucking happy."

"Wait, is this why you've been avoiding intimacy with me?"

"Hell yeah. The first time we slept together, I bit you and bonded us, and I wanted to give you time to wrap your head around a relationship with me."

"What am I to you?" she asked suddenly.

"What?"

"Don't think. Just tell me the first word that comes to your head. What am I?"

"My mate. The shifter word for it feels right."

She blew out a relieved breath and grinned at him. "Okay then, mate. You can talk to me about this stuff. You're a vampire. And yeah, it weirded me out at first, but it is what it is. You eat what you eat. Hiding that part of yourself from me won't help us. It'll keep me at a distance, and I don't want that."

"What do you want?"

"All of you. I want it all—the good, the bad, everything." Crossing her arms over her chest, she admitted, "I like brussels sprouts."

The tension faded from Aric's rigid profile as he pulled into her driveway. "Well, liking vegetables and liking blood are different."

"I also like my steak rare. It's the leopard in me. Walk my cow past the fire, and I'm good."

Aric slid his strong hand over her thigh and squeezed her gently, then gave her that sexy crooked grin he'd been sharing more and more lately. Faint dimples bracketed his sensual lips right now. God, he was stunning.

"Thanks for understanding. I'll call one of the girls tomorrow then."

"Or..." She waggled her eyebrows. *Hint, hint, hint.*

"Or what?" he asked in a careful tone. Were his eyes growing even darker now?

Sadey gave him a flirty grin and flounced out of her car, then sashayed up the walkway toward her front door. She could smell him following but couldn't hear his footsteps, and when she looked over her shoulder, he was practically floating behind her with a drunken look in his hungry eyes. She unlocked the door and stepped into her living room, now unpacked and in order again.

Aric stopped at the door, rested his palms on either side of the door frame. She hadn't invited him in yet so he was good and stuck.

Slowly, she pulled her sweater over her head and draped it across the back of the couch, her eyes never leaving his. Sadey adored the way he looked at her, as if she was the most beautiful creature he'd ever laid eyes on. He made her feel like a goddess. With a wicked grin, she shimmied out of her shoes and jeans. Then she locked one arm against the couch, poking out her hip so he could enjoy all her curves.

Aric's hungry eyes raked down her body, pausing on the hot spots. He blinked slowly and lifted that roiling black gaze back to her. That crooked smile was back.

"Do you *want* to come in?" she asked, teasing him with the almost-invite.

He nodded once, and now she purred under his sexy stare. Anticipation zinged up her spine as she parted her lips and whispered, "Aric, won't you come in?"

His form dissolved into a cloud of bats and smoke and then, in an instant, he was solid again right in front of her, driving her backward as the door slammed behind him hard enough to rattle the room.

She gasped as her back hit the wall and his long, thick erection pressed against the apex of her thighs. His lips were on her now, moving against hers like water, so hard his elongating teeth were grazing her tender skin with every stroke of his tongue.

"Oooh," she moaned. He linked their hands, then shoved them up the wall above her head.

Sadey arched her back against the wall, desperate to be closer to him. In a moment, he released her hands and tore his shirt off, undid his pants, and rolled his hips against hers. Her panties made a soft *riiiip*, and then they were on the floor with his shirt and, oh Mylanta, she'd never gone from revved up to inferno this fast before.

He made a low, wild sound deep in his throat as he pulled the backs of her knees up around his waist and slid into her. Resting his head against her shoulder, he froze when he hit her clit. "God, you feel so good," he gritted out. He eased back and then shoved into her again, and again. Faster as the pressure of blinding pleasure expanded in her middle. He was so big, so thick, filling her. Sadey hugged him desperately, sank her nails into his back because he was slamming into her hard now, and she was so close.

"Aric," she whispered, arching her head back and exposing her neck.

He hugged her waist tight, pulled her against him as he stayed deep, pumping into her. He let off a needy sound as he kissed her neck, dragging his fangs across her skin in a delicious tease.

"Do it!" she cried as the first pulse of orgasm exploded through her.

His teeth were so sharp she didn't feel them enter

her skin. Not as he bucked into her, conjuring every pounding aftershock. She pressed her hand against his throat just to feel him swallowing. He froze, and wet heat throbbed into her. He reared his hips back and then rocked against her again. Over and over, his shaft swelled and pulsed as he emptied himself

His grip around her ribs tightened as he drank her. *"It's okay. Almost done. So good."*

And just as her fingers began to tingle with cold, he unlatched from her neck and sucked gently on her skin until her shifter healing sealed the cuts. Their heaving chests matched in rhythm. She gripped the back of his hair tightly, unwilling to let him go yet. Her breath shook at how intense and amazing that had been, and when Aric pulled back and lifted his gaze to hers, his eyes had softened to a dark gray.

"Are you okay?" he murmured, concern flashing across his face.

Sadey smiled, and unable to find her voice yet, she nodded.

Aric's relief was instant. It came off him like a gust of wind. He carried her gingerly into her bedroom and crawled under the sheets with her, pulled her tight against his chest, and let his lips linger on top of her hair.

She clung to him and stared at the window. The sky was lightning on the horizon, and the sunlight would chase away her love soon. Her love? Sadey pressed a soft kiss against his chest and smiled. Yeah, that word felt right. She loved him.

"Sadey?"

"Mmm?" she asked dreamily as sleep tugged at her body.

He lowered his lips to her ear and whispered, "You're reaching again."

"Okay," she murmured as her eyelids grew heavier. How could she feel this safe in someone's arms?

"Can I tell you something?" he asked softly.

"You can tell me anything."

He kissed her gently, a slight smile on his lips as he did. And when he eased back, he brushed his knuckle against her cheek and whispered, "I love you, too."

EIGHT

Sadey startled awake. She blinked rapidly, her heart galloping against her sternum. The soft glow of the living room light fixture made her wince. She'd fallen asleep on the couch, and the television now had a frozen screen, asking if she was done watching the show she'd nodded off to.

She exhaled and stretched, then smiled as Aric cupped her breast and settled again. Silly mate, feeling her up in his sleep.

Sleep? She frowned at the window near the door. It was still pitch black outside.

Her blood chilled to ice. Aric was on shift tonight, not lying behind her on the couch. Panting shallowly in fear, she forced her gaze down to the arm draped over her hip. It was bigger than Aric's, tanned from the sun, and scarred from where she'd raked her claws down it after Brock had hit her.

"Did you miss me, baby?" Brock murmured in her ear. His warm breath made her want to retch.

She lay there, too afraid to breathe, too afraid to move, her palms going damp with sweat. Her animal snarled a warning, but she couldn't get a single muscle to move when he sat up and pressed his weight onto her, slipped his meaty hand around her throat.

It was the touch of his calloused hand against her skin that woke the fight in her. Sadey struggled like some wild thing, but Brock was twice her weight. She wanted to Change, but he was straddling her now, both hands wrapped around her throat, his eyes glowing the same light gold color hers did. Sadey thrashed and bucked, gasping for air, but Brock's eyes were empty. They were soulless.

"I knew you were here all along, you stupid bitch," Brock growled out. "Who do you think ran you off the road? Who do you think has been watching you play house with that fucking bloodsucker? I was going to let you live, Sadey." His voice echoed with the hollowness of insanity. "If you would've come back to me, I would've let you live."

"Please," she choked out. "Don't." Tears streamed down the corners of her eyes. She wasn't ready to go yet. Wasn't ready to succumb to the darkness without telling Aric goodbye. Without explaining she'd tried to be stronger for him.

"You'll die alone now. No people, no friends. No vampire fuck-buddy to save you. He's working. He'll find your body long after you've gone cold, and that's my revenge on him for taking what was mine. I can put you in the grave, and he can't raise you from the dead."

Wait...Aric. Reach! *"Aric! Help me! Please, Aric."* She squeezed her eyes closed against the shattering edges that were demolishing her vision. Sparks zipped this way and that behind her eyelids as she sucked desperately for air. *"Aric...I'm sorry. I love you. I'm sorry."*

This was it. The end. The darkness had reached across two state lines and swallowed her up. At least she'd had a good ending. A happy one. How sad would it have been to go still trapped?

The front of her house exploded inward, and

when she opened her eyes, sheetrock, siding, insulation, and glass blasted above Brock. His face was red with hate and exertion, but as he looked up, fear flashed in his eyes. And then he was gone.

There was no weight pressing her down, no hands crushing her neck. There was just the beautiful breath of oxygen she dragged into her lungs, and then the pain of her knees hitting the wood floor beside the couch.

Aric was against the wall, and a moment of confusion took her. Where was Brock?

Aric reached in the hole and yanked something massive out of it. Brock fell to his knees, crimson painting his neck and arm.

Sadey winced away from the sight of Brock's throat, which had been badly torn. Gads, Aric was so much faster and more lethal than she'd realized.

The front of the house was demolished, and outside, the *squeak, squeak* of bats and a thick purple haze transformed the night. Garret appeared on the porch first, and then one by one, the rest of the Asheville coven solidified.

Aric paced wordlessly, only a deep hiss in his throat as his eyes stayed on Brock who was hunched over and holding his bleeding neck.

"Sadey, are you okay?" Garret asked from outside.

She tried to say yes, but couldn't get her voice box to work yet, so she nodded instead. Swallowing hard, she wheezed out, "Come in. All of you come in."

Garret stepped over the rubble, followed by the others. When he helped her upright, his hand was strong and cold and firm under her elbow. His jet black eyes churned with hatred as he looked at Brock. Then to Aric, he said, "Kill him for what he's done."

What? Sadey thought the coven hated her, but here was Aric's Second encouraging vengeance against crimes committed against her.

Aric shook his head hard as though he couldn't think straight. "It's your right," he ground out, casting a quick, dark glance to Sadey. "Do you want to kill him? Or do you want me to take the burden. I can. I want to."

But did she want that? Did she want to make Aric a murderer? He cared about life so much—human, shifter, and vampire. Would killing Brock ease his need to defend her, or would it hurt him?

"There's another way to keep him out of our

lives." She punched each word past her vocal chords, and it hurt, but this needed to be said. "There's a way that would keep the blood off both of our hands."

In a moment, Aric's face transformed to that of realization. His lips snarled back over his long, sharp fangs, as though a part of him still wanted to end Brock's life. But Aric wasn't like Brock. He wasn't heartless, and the more she thought about it, the more she knew Aric would carry this night with him for always if she didn't keep logical enough for both of them.

"I want him dead for what he did to me, Aric. I do. But a quick death is too easy on him and will echo through this coven for always." She swallowed hard and clenched her fists. "Wreck him instead."

Aric's snarl turned to an empty smile, and he squatted down just out of Brock's reach. Brock stretched his hand for him, but when Aric twitched his chin, Brock reared back as if he'd been slapped. And then Brock's bright blue eyes were taken over with the dark color of his pupils as they dilated completely.

She didn't want to watch, so she followed Garret and the others outside. A few of them asked if she was all right and wanted to know what had happened. She tried to explain in as few words as possible, her gaze never far from the inside of her house where Aric was canting his head the other way, his eyes locked on Brock's as he put who-knew-what visions into his head.

Brock looked terrified, his eyes wide, his mouth hanging open like he was mid-scream. She'd never seen fear on his face until tonight. She tried to conjure a single ounce of pity for him, but couldn't. He would've killed her with his bare hands while he stared at her petrified face if Aric hadn't come for her.

Aric was talking low now, murmuring something not even her snow leopard hearing could pick up.

"Sheeeyit," Garret muttered in a gleeful voice, shaking his head. "Our king isn't playing around. This guy's fucked." He turned to her and frowned thoughtfully. "I hoped Aric's interest in you would pass. It won't, will it?"

Sadey rubbed her tender neck and shook her head. "I hope not."

"Do you love him?"

Her voice pitched to a whisper as soft as a breath as she answered, "I do. Very much. Garret, how did you know to come here?"

He chuckled darkly. "Your man pulled in the entire coven. It wasn't our choice. Looks like we owe you fealty now."

"I'm sorry."

"Don't say that, shifter. Don't let the boys see a drop of weakness, or they'll test you relentlessly. Apologize for nothing. It's beneath you."

"Beneath me?" she whispered, staring at the other vamps who stood in pairs talking low.

Garret leveled her with a look, one eyebrow cocked, his chin lifted high. "You're mated to the King of the Asheville Coven now, Sadey. Chest up, chin out, princess. You are royalty in our coven."

"Our coven," she murmured.

She'd never been a part of anything like this. These almost strangers had come to help her. Even if Aric had forced them, Garret had showed her kindness tonight, and the others, too.

Perhaps she'd been wrong about vampires. Perhaps it wasn't just Aric who was protective and caring.

Inside, Aric stood and crossed his arms over his fire department shirt, puffing out his biceps and chest with the motion. He tracked Brock's progress as her ex left the house. Brock shook uncontrollably and looked around like a terrified field mouse in the shadow of an owl. When his eyes landed on her, Brock screamed a high pitched, horrified sound. He pinned himself against the porch railing, chest heaving as he sobbed.

"Go on, or I'll let her have you," Aric said blandly.

Shoulders shaking with his crying, Brock ran for his car, tripped in the yard, and then crawled as fast as he could through the mowed grass. The murmur of the coven's chuckling filled the night as Sadey watched Brock blast out of the driveway in the black pickup truck that had run her off the road. He must've bought it recently, but if he wasn't careful, he was going to swerve off the road himself.

She turned around to ask Aric what he'd put in Brock's head, but he was right there, and he hugged her so tightly it pushed the air out of her lungs. His face was buried against her neck, and she could feel it—the relief.

"Are you okay? Tell me you're all right, Sadey. I heard you…fuck." He hugged her tighter, lifted her off the ground. "I heard you call for me, and I was afraid I would be too late. I heard you say you were sorry." His voice hitched on that last word. "Garret," he said in a hard tone as he set her down.

"Yep, we're on it," Garret muttered. "Come on boys, let's check out the damage." The others meandered up onto the porch, but Garret hung back and clapped his king on the shoulder. "I'll order the supplies, and we'll get it fixed up."

"Thank you," Aric murmured to Garret's back as his Second made his way up to the destroyed house with the others.

Cupping her face and angling it back, he studied her throat. His relief she'd felt a second ago transformed to anger, and power pulsed against her skin. "I wanted to kill him, Sadey. Seeing him choking you…" He gritted his teeth and looked like he wanted to spit. "You should know what's in my heart. If you hadn't spoken up for him, that asshole wouldn't be breathing right now."

"I wasn't speaking up for him, Aric."

Her mate frowned, and confusion filled every beautiful angle of his face. "What do you mean?"

"I was speaking up for *you*." Sadey gripped Aric's wrists to keep his touch on her. "I didn't want you to have another black mark on your heart because of me. I wanted to protect you."

Deep emotion pooled in his eyes as he shook his head in disbelief. "I keep thinking you're a dream. Like I'll wake up, and my life will be like it was before you. Dark and empty. I don't know how I got lucky enough for you to pick me back." He parted his lips to say more, but his phone chirped in his back pocket. He checked it and muttered a curse. "I have to get back to the station. Will you do me a favor?"

"Well, you did just save my life," she said with a shaky laugh. "I pretty much owe you any favor you want. What'll it be? Titty squeezes? A BJ? I'm drawing the line at a threesome because I don't share my man, my food, or—"

Aric kissed her into silence, making her forget her train of thought completely. With a deep chuckle, he eased back and rested his forehead against hers. "I was just going to ask you to sleep at the coven house tonight. My protective instincts are kicked up, and Garret can make sure you are comfortable." He bit his bottom lip and grinned wickedly. "We can discuss BJ negotiations when I get home."

"Deal," she whispered, thoroughly enjoying the

way he'd said *home*, as if it was hers, too.

But as she watched him saunter off, evaporate into a powerful gust of bats and smoke, and then disappear into the night, she reconsidered that word. Home wasn't her rental house or the coven house, or even Winterset.

Now, home was Aric.

NINE

Aric smiled at the new bed of flowers in the landscaping of the coven house. Three months living here, and Sadey had put her stamp on every piece of this place. The music of laughter floated out of the open windows and reached for him on the front porch.

This was his favorite part of his fire shifts—when he got to come home to her and to his coven.

His old life felt a million years ago now.

Aric pushed open the door and paused in the entryway just long enough to set his gear bag down. Dawn was an hour away, but the boys were still riled up, joking with each other and playing the music too loud. Quietly, Aric padded into the living area and leaned against the doorframe there. Dawn and the girls were here tonight, which made the human food smell of steak make sense. Sadey always insisted on cooking for the feeders before they left so they wouldn't feel faint on the way back to their lives.

The coven had complained half-heartedly at first about cooking in the kitchen and filling the house with the stink of food, but Sadey wouldn't be budged, and Aric was glad. The feeders were happier for the tradition they were creating now. Dawn and Sadey were cracking up over something at the table as his mate forked a bite of salad. She had her blond tresses up in a messy bun and wore an easy smile that said she was comfortable with everyone here. Her charcoal gray cable-knit sweater dropped from one shoulder and exposed the claiming mark he'd given her.

Some of the coven were on the couch watching a television show, two were playing chess in the corner, and two of them were sitting at the table with the girls, teasing them. Garret was standing over the old jukebox the boys had ordered for the house, and after he punched in the number he wanted, Sadey groaned out, "Garret! We've heard this song three thousand times tonight."

"And we'll hear it three thousand more because it's that good," he said with a wink at Dawn.

These were Aric's favorite nights, when everyone was happy.

"Hey you."

Aric blinked slowly and smiled at his mate. Sadey looked so pretty under the chandelier above the kitchen table, an easy greeting grin on her full lips, her eyes crinkling as the grin reached them.

She really loved him.

Sure, he could tell from the fact that she'd switched her work hours and sleep schedule around to coincide with his. He could tell from the way she snuggled him in her sleep in the dark of their room during the daylight hours. But this—the way she looked at him with her heart in her eyes—said she was happy to be in love with him.

He twitched his chin toward the hallway, and her smile deepened. She squeezed Dawn's shoulder as she passed and made her way to him.

"I missed you," she murmured as she snuggled into his arms. And then she rested her cheek against his chest and went to purring like she always did when he came home after a shift.

He lifted her chin, brought her gaze to his so she would see how much he meant his next words. "I missed you, too." And then he leaned down and kissed her, his hands sliding down her neck and arms until he reached her waist.

She was always so reactive to his touch, and then she was reaching again. "*Love, love, I love him, love him. I love Aric.*"

He chuckled and nipped at her lip. His mate was a loyal creature who loved with her whole heart, and she'd somehow chosen him. He was so damn lucky to have landed in Winterset. So damn lucky to have landed in Sadey's arms.

"Get a room," Garret called across the couch.

Fine by him. Aric waved goodnight to his coven and hugged his mate tightly as he walked her backward down the hallway.

Sadey wrapped her legs around his waist. "Night, vamps," she called over his shoulder.

"Night." The coven's murmurs bounced down the hallway after them as Aric maneuvered them down the stairs to the basement rooms.

"Tell me about your day, mister," she murmured,

resting her chin on his shoulder.

Aric kicked open the door to their bedroom and closed it with his hip, then murmured, "It was an easy one. No calls. The town was quiet tonight. And Chief Lang pulled me in his office at the end of my shift."

"What for?" she asked as he settled her onto the wood floor.

Aric shook his head, still barely able to believe it himself. "He said I was an asset to the truck and he'd made the right decision in hiring me."

Sadey's beaming smile stunned him into stillness. "So are you still the King of the Asheville Coven?" she asked innocently.

He could see it clear as day what she wanted him to say. He'd balked before tonight, but now it felt right. "No. Now I'm the King of the Winterset Coven."

"So we're staying. Officially, this is home?"

The excitement in her voice was catching, and he laughed. With a nod, he murmured, "We're home."

The notes of Garret's favorite country song floated down through the ceiling. Aric held Sadey as gently as she deserved and rocked them side-to-side in a slow dance. Resting his cheek against her hair, he murmured, "Before I met you, I was so angry. I couldn't get over Arabella stealing the sunlight from me. I couldn't be the king I wanted to be because of my unhappiness with her betrayal."

Sadey clutched his shirt and sighed, relaxing against him as they slow-danced. "And now?"

He leaned back and searched her gorgeous eyes. Slowly, he pressed his hand over her chest where her content purr rattled on. "And now I think I was supposed to find you when I did because you banished the dark parts of my life right when I thought I would be lost."

She was flowers in the garden and secret smiles. She was love, happiness, and echoing laughter. Somehow, she'd come in and become the glue for his coven—the glue for the pieces of himself Aric thought he had lost.

After everything, she had chased the shadows away, and now he didn't have to mourn his old life or the things he'd had to give up.

Because Sadey—his fiercely beautiful, playful, tender-hearted Sadey—had turned out to be his sunlight.

T. S. JOYCE
SECOND OF THE
Winterset
COVEN

Second of the Winterset Coven

(Winterset Coven, Book 2)

PROLOGUE

NORWAY, 904

Geir Westergaard searched the village but didn't see her anywhere. Torunn wasn't among the farewell crowd at the docks, and she wasn't at the market that lined the main road either.

"Your woman forget what today is?" Gunnar asked, shoving him in the shoulder.

Geir shoved him back hard, debating whether to nick the bastard with his blade for even touching him. Gunnar had been pushing him too far lately. "She'll be here."

A long bellow of the horn sounded from the top of the cliffs where the chieftain's first son was blowing the first warning. Fuck, he was going to miss saying goodbye.

Geir pulled his furs closer and made his way through the crowd.

"Where are you going?" Gunnar called after him. "To get your dick wet one last time?"

"Tell them not to leave without me!" Geir yelled back in their native tongue.

Behind him was chaos. It was wives and children bidding farewell to their men for the Viking raids that happened every spring. It was saying goodbye to people they might never see again if they met their end in battle. If they were called up by Odin to Valhalla.

Geir had always thought the women silly and sentimental before this raiding season, but he was different now. Everything was different. Torunn had made him soft. He'd fought it at first, but she wasn't just some good fuck to relieve him after a fight. She was his, so why the hell wasn't she here to see him off?

His fur-lined boots squished through the mud, and his breath froze in front of his face as he jogged faster. His hut was on the edge of the village, and something deep inside knew she would be there.

Geir skidded to a stop in front of his door. Torunn had hung reflective glass, but why? Probably some superstition. She was a medicine woman, and some of the townspeople feared her, but not Geir. She was a shield-maiden—tough, frightening, fearless—and he was high in the clan, so good. People should fear his woman.

His face was ferocious in the glass. His hair was shaved on the sides to reveal his tattoos, and his black hair on top was braided in thick layers that trailed down his back. His eyes were bright green and fierce, and the scars on his face and neck showed how many battles he'd fought and survived.

When a soft sniffle sounded from inside, Geir frowned.

Good at war he may be, but good at love he was not.

With his calloused hand, he shoved open the door. Torunn was sitting on his bed, hunched over, tears spilling onto her lap. Fuck. What did he do with a woman's tears?

The horn sounded again, long and steady. The Viking ships would soon push off the shore.

"Why aren't you saying goodbye to me?" he asked gruffly, kneeling in front of her.

She didn't seem surprised to see him here, and it angered him. Was this another game to get him to chase her? Torunn loved games.

"I want to go, too," she said in a trembling voice.

She'd grown weak after being injured in a fight with another clan. She'd gotten the fever from an ax slice on her back. Torrun's body had healed, but her mind had stayed weak. He missed the old Torunn, but a part of him liked her like this, too. He liked her needing him. Weakness wouldn't keep her alive, though, not with him gone across the seas. Not without him here to protect her.

"The mirror?" he asked.

"It's there to bring you back home safely. It's there so I see your reflection and know it's really you."

Nothing she'd said made any sense. Her words were like a puzzle, and he was a simple man. A war man. "I've never heard of that. Where did you learn that?"

"I dreamed of it." Suddenly, she grabbed his hands in her own and lifted those bright blue eyes to his. Her long blond braids fell forward over her shoulders with the movement. "Geir, if I can't go, you shouldn't go."

"Stop," he said, shaking her hands off and standing. "Torunn, I am the chieftain's nephew. What would you have me do? Tell them I don't feel like going on the raids this season? It doesn't work like that. It's not my choice, and even if it was, I would still go. I won't rot here waiting to die. I will die in battle and find my place in Valhalla."

"But I don't want you to die on this raid, Geir! I want to have babies before you go, and when I close my eyes, I see such terrors. Your throat covered in blood and something awful hovering over you. You won't die in battle! You'll get stuck in the in-between, Geir, and me with no babies. With nothing to remember you by. Please, don't leave," she sobbed, clutching at his hands.

Geir yanked out of her grasp. This wasn't how a Viking woman should behave. It wasn't how a shield-maiden should behave. It was beneath her. "Stop it, Torunn. I won't hear anymore. It's an honor to meet battle like this. You make me weak in the heart, but I can't give you my soul, woman. It's not yours to take, and you shouldn't ask." He spun to leave but she was crying so hard now so he paused at the door. "I'll find you again in this life or the next, I swear."

The third horn sounded and he couldn't stay any longer. He gave her one last baffled look, then ran for the ships and left his beloved behind.

ONE

"Oops," Craig said as he dumped a shot of whiskey down the front of Dawn's white shirt.

Dawn gasped and shoved the empty tray between them to shield herself. Craig spat on the floor of Trager's Bar and lifted eyes full of hatred to her. "Blood bag whore," he gritted out.

Those words stung more than any other. Blood Bag. That's what people called humans who volunteered as feeders for the covens. But this wasn't just some stranger making a snap judgement about her. She'd known Craig since high school, and he was treating her like dirt under his boots. And for what?

When his friends around the table laughed, the edges of Dawn's vision blurred with embarrassed rage. She wished she was stronger, tougher, and could come up with good words to curse them all out and make them respect her. But she wasn't that girl. All she could do was murmur, "I don't do that anymore."

Craig snorted. "Got all used up by a vamp, and now who will want you?"

The words sliced like a knife. She had loved the vamp she fed. She still did, and now she couldn't sleep, couldn't eat. She was completely cut off from the man who had stolen her heart, and Craig was being careless with his assumptions.

"Craig," her boss, Trager, warned from the next table over, "that's enough." The giant gave Craig a hard look before he went back to organizing receipts.

"You could've had me, Dawn." Craig said, his words slurring slightly. "I asked you out like ten times, and you said no. You chose a fucking corpse instead."

"Okay," Trager said, standing so fast his chair screeched across the tile floor. "Craig, shut the fuck up. Bar's closed. You and your friends need to leave." He jerked his head toward the bathrooms and told her, "Dawn, go clean yourself up. I'll clean up out here."

The venom in his voice wasn't lost on her, though. Cleaning up meant the ex-bouncer was about to bounce Craig's dumb ass right out of this bar. Trager wasn't much older than her, but he had old-fashioned manners about violence in front of women, and thank God for small blessings. She didn't want to see it. Dawn set her tray on the table and jogged to the bathroom.

She turned on the water full-blast to drown out the scuffle outside and went to scrubbing damp paper towels all over her whiskey-soaked cleavage.

The fitted white bar shirt was now stained, but that wasn't why she locked her arms against the counter and let off a long shaking breath. It wasn't why she closed her eyes tightly against the pain in her chest. She hadn't lied when she'd told Craig she didn't feed vampires anymore.

Garret had let her go. He'd let her down. He'd broken up with her. Or maybe he'd just broken…her.

They'd never even kissed. That was his rule while he fed from her neck. He was gentle with his fangs, and had seemed to like her outside of the feedings. He'd made her feel special, even flirted, but now she was questioning everything. If she really was special to him, how could he push her away so easily?

Dawn exhaled hard, blowing a flyaway lock of hair out of her face. All men left.

She blinked hard to keep the tears at bay. One quick glance in the mirror, and she wanted to shatter it with her fists, so her reflection would match her insides. She knew better than to attach to a man, but she'd thought Garret was different. Better. She'd thought he was building that slow bond that would turn into an epic love story. Her love story.

Swallowing hard, Dawn forced herself to look in the mirror so she could repeat the mantra she uttered when the heartbreak threatened to devour her. "Hold it together. You weren't wrong. You fell for a man, and there's no shame in that. Falling is good. He just wasn't there to catch you. Someday, somebody will. Your person is out there. You won't be alone forever." Her words trembled coming out. She didn't believe them yet, but if she said them often enough, maybe someday she would. And maybe someday, they would come true.

Her cheeks and nose were red, as if they'd already prepared for her to break down and cry like the wuss she was. Her eyes looked even bluer with all that red coloring, and her blond hair hung limply from her high ponytail. This last month had been hell.

Dawn washed her hands and turned off the sink, then went to work making sure the bathroom supplies were stocked so Craig would be long gone by the time she went back out there to help Trager close up the bar.

But when she finally drifted back out to the main room, Trager wasn't alone as she'd expected. The bar was small, and on most nights she and her boss could handle business, just the two of them. Trager was standing behind the bar, staring at a man who was sitting at a table in the very center of the room. Her boss didn't move a muscle or look at her when her sneakers made loud squeaky sounds on the tile floor. His eyes stared vacantly.

Dawn slowed to a stop as the hairs rose on the back of her neck. She didn't recognize the stranger, but she sure as hell recognized the tattoos that trailed down his neck into his collared shirt. She'd seen similar ones on Garret when his barber had cut his hair too short on the sides.

The man turned and slid eerie-colored gray eyes

to her. His lip twitched, and he didn't look surprised at all to see her.

His hair was long and blond like hers, but his skin was pallid and held the slight blueish hue of the unliving.

"You can't be in here," she gritted out, angry at what he was doing to Trager. "You haven't been invited in."

"Public building, and anyway, you're wrong. Trager here invited me in."

Dawn cast a quick glance at Trager, but he was still frozen against the bar. There was a stake under the register, on the shelf right near his knees, and Dawn would bet her boobs he had tried to get to it before this asshole vamp turned him into a statue.

Rage flared up through her chest. "What do you want?"

The man stood and approached slowly. "You look just like her, you know."

Dawn took a step back for every one he took toward her, as the fury in her chest transformed to fear. "L-like who?"

"Like the bride of Geir the Destroyer." His words were English, but with a slight accent she didn't recognize.

Dawn's back hit the wall, and she whimpered when his cold fingertips touched her neck as he brushed her flyaway tresses behind her shoulder.

"You can't be her though, can you? You don't smell immortal. You don't look like the eternal." He inhaled deeply and gripped the back of her neck too hard. "I can practically taste your soul. Have you finally been reborn then I wonder?" The monster's breath was cold like an arctic wind across her cheeks as he spoke, and his teeth were elongating.

"Trager," she desperately pleaded.

Over the man's shoulder, Trager was sweating as if he was fighting the vampire's hold, but he still wasn't moving.

"Tell me about Geir now. How has he changed after all this time? Does he speak of me? Does he speak of the lost and the damned? Does he dream of his origin?"

"I don't know. I don't know what you're talking about! I don't know anyone named Geir."

"Lie!" he roared, flattening her against the wall. He lowered his voice. "I can smell him on you. Say his name. Cry out for him and beg him to save you. Only one is fast enough and powerful enough to save your neck from me. Call to him. Tell him Asmund the Dark is here. Say his name."

Tears streamed from the corners of her eyes as she struggled against him with everything she had. She could see her death coming when he opened his jaws wide, exposing his white, razor-sharp teeth that shone in the dim light.

Garret, Garret, Garret. Say it! Call him to you.

Dawn inhaled and screamed, "Garret!"

And then she waited.

She waited as the monster's fangs punctured her skin.

The pain worsened with her struggle, and she cried harder. Eventually her arms and legs went cold and numb. And still she watched the door of the bar, and still she waited.

"Garret," she sobbed, growing weak.

Asmund was killing her. He was draining her, and there was a chance she would come back a vampire. She didn't want this. Not from Asmund, but Garret was going to let it happen.

Just as sparks dashed this way and that on the edge of her vision like shooting stars, the monster released her.

Dawn fell, and pain shot through her knees when she hit the unforgiving floor.

Asmund was smiling, his teeth red. She hated him.

"Good Torunn," he murmured, and then he disappeared in a thick, black fog.

Dawn locked her arms against the floor and glared at the door.

Still she waited, but Garret never came. Only Trager, who was rocking her now, holding a towel against her neck and talking fast and frantic into the phone.

And in this moment, something deep inside of her awakened. Something quiet and barely there. Something that was only a whisper against her heart.

She'd fallen for a let-down man.

TWO

Dawn made her way through the four girls waiting to feed the Winterset Coven. Three of them waved to her and said hi, but she wasn't here for niceties, and if she was honest, being here hurt. She used to be a part of this. She used to be proud to be a feeder—Garret's feeder—because silly her, she thought there had been something deeper to it.

Fine, she wasn't one of the cool kids anymore, but Garret owed her answers. She lifted her clenched fist and banged hard on the door.

Aric, the King of the Winterset Coven, opened it and frowned down at her. "Dawn?"

"I need to talk to him."

A flash of worry slithered through his dove-gray

eyes before he composed his face again and shook his head to deny her. "Sorry Dawn, we aren't ready for feeders yet."

Feeders. She hadn't ever minded that word until now.

"Then he can make time for an old friend."

Aric placed himself in front of the door, blocking her as she tried to enter.

"Let her in," Sadey Lowen, the snow leopard shifter mate of Aric, said softly from behind him. "She should see him."

"Sadey, now's not the time," he murmured low.

But Sadey shoved him back and yanked Dawn's arm until she was following her down the long hallway that led to the basement door. Before they went down, Sadey spun and hugged Dawn hard. "I wanted to come visit you at the hospital, but the police were down our throats. They tried to pin your attack on the coven." She stood back at arm's length, her gold eyes glistening. "Was it horrible?"

Dawn swallowed over and over in trying to keep her emotions in check. "I'm fine."

Sadey brushed her fingertip down the bandage on Dawn's neck and whispered, "That's a lie, and we both know it. I miss you around here. Nothing's the same. Garret's not..." Sadey inhaled deeply and squeezed Dawn's shoulders. "Dawn, before you go in there, you should know something."

Dawn frowned and gripped Sadey's wrists. She was still one of Dawn's best friends, even if Dawn wasn't welcome here anymore. "What is it?"

"He's...had a hard time since you left."

Pain unfurled in her chest at Sadey's admission. Despite what he'd done, Dawn still cared so deeply for Garret it scared her. She didn't want him to hurt, but then again, she was hurting, and him struggling was fair. At least he felt something. At least she wasn't the only one suffering. "I didn't leave, Sadey. I was pushed out. By him. Whatever hard time he's going through is self-induced. None of this was my choice." She moved out from under Sadey's grasp and shoved the basement door open, then jogged down into the darkness.

In the hallway, there was one single light, covered by a thick fixture that dimmed the illumination, but she knew this house like the back of her hand. Second door to the end was the Second of the Winterset Coven's room. Over the last two days, her roiling anger had grown so deep and wide, any warning in her mind to be wary of a big, powerful vampire was snuffed out by the little devil on her shoulder that was telling her to "fuck him up."

If her legs weren't so brittle and wimpy, she would've kicked in the door like a badass—she was that riled up. To save herself from broken knees and embarrassment, she used the door knob like a normal human and shoved it open so hard it banked off the wall. Hell yes. She opened her mouth to spew magma-hot rage at him, but at her first glimpse of Garret, the words got stuck in her throat.

He was sitting on his bed, facing away from her, head in his hands. His skin was pale in the soft light. She'd never seen him without a shirt on, and his back was covered in scars. The marks were old, silver, different widths and lengths. She'd always known Garret was muscular from the way his clothes fit him, but she hadn't expected his shoulders to be so wide and for every tensed muscle to show.

When a long hiss sounded from him, he shook his head hard to stop the sound. "I said I don't want any feeders. I'm not ready." His voice was gruff and nearly unrecognizable.

When Dawn closed the door gently behind her, Garret slid a hard glance over his shoulder. His eyes were black as pitch, and his face fearsome. He looked hungry.

When he saw her, Garret stood suddenly to his full height. Gads, she'd almost forgotten how tall he was.

"You shouldn't be here," he said, eyes on the wall, his desk, his dresser—anywhere but on her.

"I thought we were friends."

Garret huffed a breath. "Friends?"

"Don't do that," she said, approaching slowly. "Don't make me feel like I was nothing. How many hours did we spend in here, playing chess, talking, laughing? How much time did I spend with your coven—"

"My coven, not me—"

"To spend time with you, Garret! You were the draw. Surely you know that. I'm not here to beg you to make it like it was. I'm not here to plead with you to be my friend again."

"Then why are you here?"

"Because I have questions. And I want you to know you hurt me. I was attacked by someone you know, who knows you. No matter what you say, we were friends once. You owe me answers."

Garret's black gaze ghosted to her neck and away. "Look where my friendship got you, Dawn."

"Who is Asmund?"

Garret turned away from her, slammed his fists against his desk, and stood there frozen, snarling at the wall.

Not good enough. Dawn stepped closer and whispered, "Geir."

"Don't call me that."

"It's your name, isn't it?"

"Eleven hundred years ago that was my name. Eleven lifetimes ago." His dark eyes flashed dangerously when she stepped closer and he backed away, as though he couldn't stand to be near her.

She'd done the same with the monster in the bar, backed away like this. "Are you really so repulsed by me you can't stand for me to be close?"

"You don't know what you're saying. Don't know what you're talking about. Stop. Stop!" He held out his hand to keep her at arm's length. "I haven't fed, I'm fucking starving, and you come in here, looking beautiful, looking pure, looking like everything that's right, and all I want to do is drink you up. We aren't the same, Dawn!"

Dawn stomped her foot as her eyes burned. "You didn't come for me!"

"I didn't hear you."

"Bull. Shit. I was terrified. I was dying. I was calling out for you like you told me to. You told me if I ever needed you, just say your name. I tried not to. I didn't want to give that beast anything, but I wanted to live, and you never came. I wanted you to save me, but you ignored me instead."

"I couldn't hear you," he whispered raggedly.

"You could."

"Not after I broke our bond, Dawn! I was here, playing fucking cards with Sadey, completely unaware you were even in danger. You were dying, and I was playing Spades. So I ask again. Why. Are. You. Here?"

"Why are you so hungry?"

Garret angled his face away, blinked slowly, and leveled her with those shining, black eyes.

"Why?" she asked again.

"Because the other feeders don't feel right."

"Because they aren't me?"

Garret ducked his chin to his chest. "Yep. That."

"Did you care for me?"

A hesitation, and then another nod.

"As a friend?"

Garret refused to answer, and that was answer enough. No, he hadn't cared for her just as a friend. He'd cared about her as more. She hadn't imagined it.

Dawn sat heavily on the edge of his bed and sighed. Nothing was what it had seemed with him. A hundred memories hit her at once. Countless feedings where she'd desperately wanted him to kiss her like some of the other vamps did with their feeders. She'd wanted him to touch her body and soul, but he had been so careful every time. A dozen times, she'd caught him staring at her, and then he'd look away quickly. A thousand smiles that were genuine. Smiles that she'd only ever seen him give to her.

And now she was beginning to think she hadn't known Garret, or Geir, at all.

Pain throbbed in her neck when she turned her head, and she winced. The meds had worn off, and she'd forgotten to bring them with her.

Garret sat down beside her and pulled her hand

away from the bandage where she'd been absently rubbing it. "Let me see," he murmured. His voice was still too rough, and his eyes looked like a demon's, but she trusted him. She always had.

There was a soft tearing sound, and the bandages fell away. His gaze lingered on the bloody one, but he dragged his eyes back to her neck. His face twisted with anger, but his touch over the cuts was gentle, like a butterfly wing against her skin.

"I can keep them from scarring," he whispered. "It'll look like he never touched you. I can take the pain away."

Beautiful promises. Even if her insides couldn't be fixed, Garret could fix the exterior trauma. But at what cost?

"I've missed you," she whispered, sliding her hand up his arm to his knuckles where he cupped her neck. She wanted to hold him in place and never let him go, but Garret had played a steady game for the last four months. Other than a little flirting, he'd feigned disinterest. "I missed my friend. I missed the man who always made me feel better after a shitty shift, and I've been trying really hard to get over the loss of that. If you put your lips on me…if you fix me…I'll be right back where I was. I don't want to go through detox again. Do you understand what I'm saying?"

Garret drew his leg around the back of her, giving her something to lean on just like he'd always done. "You want to be my feeder again."

It was hard to concentrate with his chiseled chest and abs on display. Garret was a warrior, and those inhuman eyes that should terrify her looked so right in his face. He'd grown his hair out longer on top, but cut his hair shorter on the sides. She could almost see the tattoos. Almost. Her mouth went dry, and she swallowed so her voice wouldn't crack when she spoke. "This isn't about money. I accept it if you can't be more with me. I don't understand it, but I can't force feelings from you."

"But you *want* feelings from me?" he asked.

Unable to find her voice anymore, she nodded. God, she felt three-whiskey-shots drunk right now, but she was to blame for that. Garret didn't have extra mind control powers like his king did, or like his maker. Just brute strength.

Garret leaned closer, cradling her gently against his chest, his hand on her neck, supporting her. "What else do you want?" he whispered, his lips close to her ear.

To stay this time. For him to care for her like she cared for him. For him to take her out on a date, meet her mom, and come visit her at work. For him to stick around. For him not to push her away again after tonight. He couldn't guarantee any of that, though.

Dawn closed her eyes and rested her hand on his chest, right over where his heartbeat should've been. His pec was hard as stone, and his skin cold as winter, and the need inside of her opened a little more. "I want you to touch me."

Garret pressed forward and kissed her neck, right over the painful marks Asmund had left behind. For a moment, she thought Garret would feed right away. She thought he would be driven to take blood to sate his thirst, but he didn't. He sucked gently, then ran his tongue up her stinging skin. The burn lessened and numbed until she felt nothing but the soft, methodic strokes of his tongue.

Now he would feed, surely.

Gripping her hair, Garret rolled her neck back and dragged his lips slowly to the other side of her throat. "Do you know how long I've wanted to do this?" he murmured against her skin. "Do you know how hard it was not to touch you when I fed? How hard it was not to kiss you after?" He slid his hand between her legs and cupped her sex.

Dawn gasped and curled in on his touch instinctively. His lips were on her neck again—kissing, sucking so gently. The points of his fangs scraped her skin, and she rolled her eyes closed at how amazing it felt. Her body loved the endorphin rush he gave when he drank from her. Maybe this was an addiction. She'd started it for the money, but stayed for Garret. For how he made her feel.

More fangs, and this was it—so different from what Asmund had done to her. Garret could erase him from her mind with this kind of adoration. Maybe that's why he was doing this. Perhaps that's why he was letting himself take her farther than he ever had before.

But just as she'd convinced herself he was doing this out of pity for a broken heart, Garret eased off her neck and gripped her hair in the back. His lips an inch from hers, he froze. His eyes were black as night as he stared at her mouth, and his chest heaved with the cool breath he panted.

Just a moment of hesitation, and then he pushed forward and pressed his lips against hers.

Shock zinged through her body and landed between her legs where he dragged his palm up slowly.

Dawn softened her lips and kissed him back, closed her eyes and got lost in the wave of pleasure that every gentle suck caused. It was everything she'd imagined and so much more. His fingers entwined in her hair stayed gentle enough not to hurt, but firm enough that she felt guided and safe.

Garret lowered her to the bed and climbed slowly over her with a lithe grace that could only come from a supe. And never once did he disengage or let her go. Not until he pushed her shirt up and pulled it from her. His arm locked on the bed, rigid and strong, he dragged his gaze down to her bra and stomach. He ground his hips against hers, and she let off a soft moan as he hit her just right at the apex of her thighs. Dawn drew her fingertips up the hard curves of his arms, across his collar bones, down the line between his defined pecks, over the mounds of his abs to the button of his jeans. All the while, she waited for him to stop her. She'd almost kissed him once when she'd been all wrapped up in the endorphins from feeding him, but he'd pulled away. And that was the night he'd ended their friendship. She'd gotten too close, and he'd punished her for it.

Not tonight, though. Tonight he let her touch him how she liked. His hips twitched when she unsnapped the button, and he sighed out a trembling breath and rolled his eyes closed when she gripped his thick shaft. He was bigger than she'd imagined all the times she'd touched herself to thoughts of him.

Gracefully, he rocked his pelvis, pushing his dick into her grip. And when he opened his eyes again, they sparked with dark intensity.

Garret kicked out of his pants, exposing a long scar on his thigh. Dawn traced it as he pushed into her other hand.

"What's that one from?"

"Battle ax," he gritted out. "Fuck, grip me harder."

She did, but at the sound of his guttural groan, she wanted so much more. Releasing him, she pushed up and kissed him. It was like lighting a fuse. Garret was back on her, lips moving against hers. He bit her bottom lip, pushed his tongue against hers, then teased her tongue into his mouth, too. He was grinding hard against her now, pulling at her pants.

"Fuck my hand or fuck me," he growled. "Choose."

Her core was molten now. He'd already made her wet with a few touches, and now Garret was giving her a choice. He was offering her one mountain or the entire world, and she wanted everything.

"You," she whispered against his lips.

His mouth curved up in a wicked grin, and then their bodies jerked with the movement of him ripping her jeans down her legs. The bra and panties came off and she was laying under him vulnerable, all of her skin against all of his, and she wanted to cry with how beautiful that felt. This, right here, in this moment, was the most profound experience she'd ever had with any man. Her body had craved this for so long, and she'd thought she'd lost him. But here she was with the man of her dreams covering her body with his like a blanket, making her feel safer than she'd ever felt. Making her feel whole and adored.

Garret intertwined their fingers and pushed her hands above her head, parted her legs wider with his knee. And when he lowered back down to the cradle he'd made, poised right there, right at her wet entrance, Dawn couldn't stop the smile from stretching her lips.

Garret chuckled as though he could sense her elation and kissed her again, slower and softer this time. As he pushed his tongue past her parted lips, he slid the head of his cock into her. She was tight because, hell, she hadn't done this in a long time, and he was big. Garret didn't push too fast, but thrust into her shallowly, then deeper and deeper until she could take all of him. Slowly he pulled out, wincing as though it physically hurt to disconnect, then thrust in hard with a groan. God, it was sexy listening to that feral sound. She'd drawn that from him. Her, a little old human bartender from Winterset, and him, a powerful battle-hardened vampire.

Over her head, she squeezed his hands gently, and he responded with another kiss. He was careful not to scrape her with his elongated fangs, and when he trailed his lips down her jaw to her throat and pushed deeply into her again, Dawn arched against the mattress and cried out. He was so good at this. It was as if he knew her body and exactly what she needed. Exactly where to touch her, lick her, nip her. And he was *nipping* now. Out slow and then bucking into her hard, he plucked at her neck with his lips like he was preparing her for the bite.

She waited for a sharp pain that never came.

Garret's abs moved against her stomach as he rocked his hips and filled her again and again. When Dawn drew her knees up to give him more room, he gripped the back of her leg and the back of her neck to hold her steady as he made love to her. It wasn't the hard fuck she'd imagined from a powerful man like him. This was more. It was deeper. It was more meaningful. Garret was making her fall in love with him all over again.

Dawn was so close. The pressure of ecstasy built with every roll of his hips against hers. He stayed deep with quick thrusts, bumping faster right at her clit.

Dawn gasped and raked her nails down his back, but Garret still didn't get rough. He smiled against her neck, then eased up and watched her face as her body shattered with deep, pulsing release.

"Garret, Garret," she panted mindlessly as he bucked into her harder and faster, jarring every aftershock from her.

His grip on the back of her neck tightened as he

buried himself and froze. His dick throbbed, filling her with warmth. A feral hiss sounded from him as he reared back and slammed into her erratically. And then just as she became too sensitive, and twitched around him, he slowed, and dragged every pleasurable pulse from her body.

Emptied completely, his aftershocks done, Garret stilled, breathing hard against her. Eyes closed, he rested his forehead on hers. They stayed like that, locked together, his cold body rigid against her warm, soft one.

The strangest feeling drifted through her. It was as if her soul recognized his and was happier for being this close. It was deep satisfaction, and fireworks, and relief, and from the slight smile on his lips, she thought he must've felt the same.

THREE

Dawn lay on her stomach, arms cradled under her, watching Garret's eyes as he tracked the curve of her back with his gaze. He trailed a light touch down her spine, hooked around to the tiny rose tattoo on her ribs, and then back up.

"I didn't know you had a tattoo," he murmured.

Dawn smiled. "No one does but my mom. She went with me to get it."

"Really?"

"Her name is Rose."

"Is this for her?" he asked, tracing the pink petals.

Dawn nodded. Their conversations had always stayed shallow, but tonight, Garret was different. He was deeper. He wanted to know more. God, she hoped that meant he wanted to keep her around.

"My dad left when I was little. I barely remember him, but my mom was amazing. Hard-working, never let us go hungry, never let money get too tight. He left, and she didn't even hesitate. There were no days in bed crying or feeling sorry for herself. She'd been a stay at home mom, and I remember two days after my dad walked out, she took me with her to a job interview at the school cafeteria."

"Your school?"

"Yeah. My school. I got to see her at lunchtime every day. The kids were mean about my mom being a cafeteria lady, but I didn't give a single shit because I knew what she was doing for us. It was me and her against the world, and I was lucky. It sucked losing my dad and always feeling that rejection, but she did her best to be mother and father for me."

"She didn't ever find someone else?"

Dawn shrugged away the pain of that question. "She almost did once."

"He left?"

Dawn's eyes were beginning to burn thinking about Gary, so she scooted closer to him and changed the subject. "Tell me about your mom."

Garret huffed a breath and rolled onto his back, linked his hands behind his head and stared up at the ceiling with a slight frown. "I don't remember her."

And there was tragedy in that. How many lifetimes had it taken for him to forget the people he knew as a human? "You don't remember anything?"

Garret swallowed hard and murmured, "Sometimes I think I remember her voice. She sang this old lullaby when I was a kid. And then she sang it once when I was grown and I'd come home from battle badly wounded. She thought I couldn't hear her. By that time, her voice was old and frail, but still had the same tone." He swallowed hard and sang a string of guttural sounding words in a language she didn't recognize. His voice was rich and deep, but broke on the last word.

"What does it mean?"

"It doesn't translate well. I don't remember any of it but that line in her voice. Maybe because I had been clinging to life so hard the last time she sang it, I don't know. Means… 'And my boy will be a man someday, a man, but I'll always love the boy, my boy.'"

Chills rippled across her skin, and Dawn snuggled against his ribs.

"My mother was there when I got my tattoos, too," he said with a sad smile. "The chieftain, too, my uncle." He traced his head in a slow arc from his temple to the base of his skull, but his hair was too long for Dawn to see them. "I got the tattoos to tell the stories of the battles I'd fought. I wanted to remind Odin of my bravery so he would let me into Valhalla when I died in battle." Garret gave his attention to the rafters again. "They're all waiting for me."

"Who?" she asked softly.

"My family. My friends. My people. They'll be waiting for all eternity. Asmund made sure I would always be severed from them."

Dawn's heart was breaking. It felt like it was ripping in two at the desolation in Garret's voice. He should've died centuries ago with the people he loved in life. She hated the thought of him long-dead in a grave, but that was how it was supposed to be. She and Garret should've never met, but just the thought of how empty her life would've been without him was unbearable. She hated Asmund, but a selfish part of her was glad he gave Garret time to make it to this moment, with her. She was sick with herself.

"Why did Asmund choose you?"

"Loneliness. Selfishness. He wanted a son. He wanted to make a man into a monster just like him so he wouldn't feel so bad about the things he did to hurt people. I left my mother, my woman, my village to go on the spring raids. I was high in our village, trusted by the chieftain, trusted by the king. I had proven myself and was confident in battle. Fearless. Stupid. I took risks to protect others. I was ruthless."

"Geir the Destroyer," she whispered, repeating Asmund's words.

"That was the name I was given, and I was proud of it. My family was proud of it. My woman knew what was going to happen. Torunn refused to say goodbye, and I was angry with her for asking me to stay. The raids were an honor. Dying was an honor, but she told me I was going to die and I wouldn't see Valhalla. I was pissed. When I left, she was sobbing. I told her I would come back for her." Garret swallowed hard and looked sick. "And I did."

"But you were a vampire?"

A slow nod. "We got blown off course in a bad storm and landed on the shore of a place we hadn't drawn on our maps. There was war, but not with humans. These men were feral, and they changed into monstrous beasts with fangs and fur, and their eyes were soulless. We were slaughtered by werewolves. I was laying in this field of carnage, bleeding, dying, fighting for every breath and pleading to Odin to take me faster. I'd been bitten over and over, ripped up, and had to hold my insides in place. Some of the bodies around me were twitching, Changing into the monsters that had killed us. Most of us died, but some did not, and I could feel it, too. My blood was like fire in my veins, and there was something growing inside of me. Something dark. The wolves were howling all around us, like they were calling their new brethren. And I remember chanting, 'Don't let me turn into one of them. Don't let me.' The howling stopped, just…cut to nothing, and I couldn't feel them there anymore, the pack. They were running away, but in their place, something else approached. Something worse."

"Asmund?"

Garret nodded slightly. "He said he would keep the wolf from eating me. I couldn't think straight. It was like he was in my head, and the pain was getting worse. He told me he would save me from the pack, and that I could go back to Torunn. He knew her name. He pulled it from my mind, and I knew I was in the presence of evil, but it hurt so bad. Everything hurt, and I wasn't dying. I could feel my body mending itself, but my insides felt like fire. I was straining, screaming, begging him to kill me before I Changed into a wolf. 'Just kill me,' I was chanting mindlessly. And he did. He drained me, and I went easy, staring up at the sky. But four days later I woke up a creature of the night, thirsting for blood like a man in the desert thirsts for water. Vampyr. That's what my terrifying childhood stories had called them, and I was that creature now. I was angry. I was Asmund's first monster, and he thought I would be like a son to him. But I hated him. Hated him for everything he'd done. I'd asked him to kill me, and he'd given me eternal life instead. It took me two years of working, of hating Asmund and refusing his urgings, to give into my instincts, but as soon as I could control the hunger and travel, I went back home. I went back to Torunn because she had been right. I thought she was the weak one, but it was me. I was a slave to the thirst now, and my instinct was to kill everything with a pulse. To drain everything alive to make myself feel better, so it was me who was the weak one. I went back home because I thought maybe she could fix me." His voice sounded hollow and heartbroken now.

"Did you kill her?" Dawn asked in horror.

"No. She killed me instead."

Dawn slipped her arms around his waist and rested her cheek on his chest. "How?"

"I reached my old home, and everything had changed. The village was quieter without all the men. The market was smaller, and everything was coated with sadness. Torunn had put reflective glass all around my cabin, not just on the door, and I couldn't see myself. I was nothing. I remember waving my hand in front of the mirrors and thinking she'd bewitched them. It was deep in the night, and I pushed open the door, but I couldn't go inside. It wasn't my home anymore and I wasn't invited. I could see her laying in my bed, under my furs, in the arms of another. She'd always wanted babies, and I hadn't given them to her, and she'd taken another husband. I was stuck, and she had moved on."

Dawn squeezed her eyes tightly closed at the pain slashing through her chest. "Asmund said I look like her. Is that why you approached me?"

"No. That's why I encouraged Aric to move the entire fucking coven here. You look just like her, and I couldn't stay away. I tried, but there has been no one since Torunn. It's like my heart latched onto her, because she was the last good thing I could remember from my human life. And in that two years I was fighting for control to be able to get back to her, she was the only thing that kept me from turning into the monster Asmund wanted me to be. There have been empty fucks, but nothing deeper, do you understand?"

"Yes," she whispered. Slowly, Dawn sat up and gave him her back as she sat on the edge of the bed. "I'm not her, Garret." She cast him a look over her shoulder. "You aren't Geir the Destroyer anymore, and I'm not Torunn, and this isn't a repeat of your love story with her. My feelings for you are my own. I don't want to be your replacement Torunn. I want to be your Dawn."

Garret huffed an amused sound. "It took me all of thirty seconds to realize you weren't Torunn reborn, Dawn. You're nothing like her. You have her looks, but you were never her replacement. The first time you told me your name, do you remember?"

She giggled and turned on the bed, drew her knees up. "You laughed at me, and I was mad. I called you a butthole. I thought you were rude for making fun of my name."

"It was just ironic to me. I am the night, and your name is Dawn, and we couldn't be any more different, you and I. It was like fate telling me to back the fuck off you, and I couldn't. I watched you serving drinks that night."

"I remember. You sat in the corner booth and barely drank anything. I felt your eyes on me the entire shift. I figured out what you were when one of the guys got too handsy and your eyes turned black."

"I wanted to kill him. I came home and asked Aric if I could."

"You did?"

Garret chuckled. "Yeah. I found out his name and everything. That asshole didn't know it, but he was stalked hard for a couple weeks before Aric laid down the law and ordered me to let him be. It's why I stopped coming to visit you at work. My protective instincts are a little ridiculous around you, and Aric told me I needed to let you alone, too. And then you showed up to be a feeder."

"I couldn't stop thinking about you," Dawn admitted. "And then there was this ad in the paper to be a feeder for your coven, and the money was good. I could help my mom pay off some of her debt with my shifts at the bar and the extra from feeding. The big draw was the thought of seeing you again, though. You terrified me, but at the same time, you excited me. You wouldn't have hurt me."

"How did you know that?" he whispered, suddenly serious.

"It was the way you said goodbye that first night. You made sure not to interrupt me while I was working, but when Trager went to shut the bar down, you approached me slowly, and you were trying to hide your eyes from me. You seemed nervous, and it didn't make sense because you're"—she waved her hand at his sculpted torso and striking face—"you. You could've had any girl in this town with a look, but you were almost shy around me. And do you remember what you said?"

Garret nodded, and his sexy smile was back. "I told you if you ever needed anything, call my name."

"I was so stunned by what you'd said. I asked you what your name was, and you leaned in slowly, gripped my shoulders, and whispered your name in my ear. It sounds crazy, but I'd never felt so safe. I thought surely it was some power you vampires had to get humans to trust you with their necks, but I couldn't get that fluttery warm feeling out of my head after you left. I wanted to feel it again, so I showed up for the feeder interviews and requested you because I just knew down to my bones you wouldn't hurt me. And you didn't until the day I tried to kiss you."

Garret shook his head. "That's not why I pushed you away, Dawn."

"Then what was it? What did I do wrong?"

"Do you remember what else happened that night?"

Dawn shook her head and suddenly felt cold just thinking about it.

"You'd downloaded that Vampire Pics app on your phone. The special one that allows you to pick up my image? You took a picture of us."

"You were my best friend. I wanted to be able to see you on the days I wasn't feeding you."

"But you posted it online, and that night I could feel him—Asmund. I'd been blocking him out of my head, keeping him off my trail, but I could feel him getting closer, and I knew it was that picture that did it. I didn't push you away because I wanted to, D. Doing that...seeing the hurt in your eyes...that hurt worse than the wolf that was growing in me all those years ago. Your friendship meant more than I can explain, and I felt awful ripping our bond from my soul. Or maybe where my soul was supposed to be. I almost felt like I had one with you. I couldn't repay you by putting you in Asmund's path. I begged Aric to move the coven just to protect you, but he's settled here. So is Sadey. So is everyone else. I was trying to protect you, not hurt you."

"Why didn't you just tell me all this?" she whispered. "I would've understood."

"Would you? You are Torunn's lookalike. How could I explain that in a way that wouldn't hurt you? How could I tell you I'd hunted you for the way you look? That I'd been hunting you for centuries, always looking for your face in crowds? How could I make you understand that I care about you for more than your face now?"

Dawn's stomach curdled, and she shrugged helplessly. "I guess that's the hard part, right? Now it's up to me. Do I believe you and trust your feelings aren't just some wish that I was someone else? Or do I cut and run. I guess I have to decide which one hurts the least. Garret?"

"Yeah?"

"Why didn't you feed from me tonight?"

He huffed a breath like it should've been obvious. "You were hurt by Asmund. It wasn't a consensual feeding, Dawn. He forced you just to get to me. I don't want to hurt you more."

"But you're thirsty."

Garret gritted his teeth. "No amount of thirst could make me hurt you when you're feeling raw like this. I'll hold. You'll heal. We'll talk about feeding later."

And there it was. He was starving—it was in his shining black eyes and the wildness of his face. She could see it in the fangs that hadn't dulled the entire time they talked. But he would rather sit this close to her in torture than hurt her.

And she trusted him. She trusted that Garret had figured it out, that she was no Torunn.

This care wasn't for a ghost of his past, but was just for her.

He may have hunted for Torunn, but he had fallen

for Dawn.

FOUR

Garret opened the door for Dawn and ghosted a glance at the lightening sky. It was a deep gray now, and sunrise would be here soon. He hated this—the fear of the sun. Some days it was enough to drive him mad.

He was wearing a pair of gray sweatpants and nothing else. Usually he hid his scars, but what was the point now? Dawn had seen all of him and hadn't seemed to mind at all. She turned on the porch and hooked her fingers in the elastic waistband that hung low on his hips. Her smile was shy and soft, and for the hundredth time he was struck with how different she'd turned out to be. He'd been convinced that Torunn would be reborn, but she hadn't been. Or if she had been, he never found her. Dawn was soft and sweet, cute and bubbly, where Torunn had been sharp as a blade and ready to battle at any moment. He used to think he needed a hard woman, but then he'd met Dawn, and she'd breathed new life into him.

Garret lifted her hand to his lips and kissed her on the inside of her thumb. God he wanted to drink her, but not until she was fully recovered.

As if she could hear his thoughts, she whispered, "Don't take another feeder. I don't like the thought of your lips on them. If you need to drink, come find me."

She was so pretty in the early morning light— the ends of her blond hair lifted in the breeze, her lips swollen from kissing him, cheeks rosy, eyes hooded and sleepy, their color like the daytime sky. It was the closest to a midday sky he would ever get. She was wearing a pair of worn, pink flip-flops and one of his T-shirts over her jeans. He'd always liked that about her—she could dress down and be comfortable in her skin and still look fucking gorgeous. Soft spoken she may be, and sweet to boot, but she was also confident, and there was nothing sexier on a woman than confidence.

"Why are you smiling at me like that?" she asked, intertwining their fingers and clasping their hands together as she shifted her weight closer.

"It's just nice to finally touch you how I want."

"You could've before."

But she was wrong. He'd been on the fence before, confused by her resemblance to Torrun, wary of his dangerous life and the effect it could have on her, worried about putting a long shadow on her life. Garret had always been careful at decisions of the heart, and he'd wanted to make sure he was all the way in before he asked her to attach to him.

Thoughts of shadows stole the smile from his face. "Do you work tonight?"

"No. Trager wanted me to take some time off while I heal up. I told him I'm fine. I could use the money. My mom has rent due soon, and I need to help her out."

Garret frowned. "Why do you have to pay for your mom?"

Dawn shrugged. "It's what family does. She's got a busted knee and has been doing physical therapy. She's recovering, but not fast enough for her job. I'm floating us until she can find another one that isn't so physically demanding."

"So you're paying your rent and hers?"

"No." She gave him a cute, little frowny smile. "Didn't you know I live with my mom?"

Garret huffed a laugh. "No. Momma's girl, huh?"

She giggled and pushed him in the shoulder playfully. Her touch was like goose down, but he allowed her to push him back so she wouldn't feel weak. "I had my own place, but she needs help. It's part of the reason I came to every feeding invite, smart aleck. That and your cute butt. *Honk*." She squeezed it, and her cheeks flushed a pretty pink color as she ducked her gaze. God, she was so fucking adorable.

"Hmm," he said nonchalantly. He had plenty of money to help her out, but something told him Dawn wasn't one to take charity or to be a kept woman. He would have to negotiate a higher wage when she fed him and hope it helped. "Go out with me tonight."

Dawn jerked her startled gaze to his. "What?"

The sky was lightening by the second, and he didn't have a lot of time to do this properly. "Go on a date with me. I want to take you out somewhere nice. Somewhere I can show you off." And somewhere in public where Asshole Asmund wouldn't dare approach them. Garret knew all that sneaky bastard's tricks.

Dawn fidgeted with the hem of her T-shirt. "Okay. What should I wear?"

He grinned. "You'll look beautiful in anything. Surprise me—*oomf*."

Garret rocked backward with the force of her hug. Startled, he lifted his hands to her back, careful to be gentle with her fragile human skin as he hugged her. She was shorter than him, so he rested his chin on top of her hair like he'd always wanted to do when she'd given him quick hugs goodbye. Fuck, this felt good. It felt good to just stand here and breathe in her scent—fruit shampoo and sex. He could smell himself on her, and he loved it. But after a few seconds, her shoulders jerked, and a soft sniffle sounded from her.

Confused, Garret eased her back to arm's length, but she wouldn't meet his eyes, and now her cheeks were even rosier. "What's wrong, woman?"

"I'm happy."

Garret was horrified. "You cry when you're happy?" He would never understand women.

"It's just, when I came here last night, I thought I

would tell you off and then it would be like before, and I would be alone again. But it's not like that. Now you feel like..."

Garret leaned down to eye level with her. "I feel like what?"

"You feel like mine. You aren't pushing me away."

"Dear God," he muttered, pulling her against his chest again and sighing in relief. "I thought I broke you."

Dawn laughed thickly and dug her little harmless claws into his lower back as she hugged him probably as tight as she could. It was like embracing a butterfly. He would have to remember to always be careful with her.

The sky had lightened to dove gray now, and any moment the sun would peek its head over the horizon. Sleep was pulling at his body, making him feel drugged. "I'll pick you up at dusk. Don't let anyone but me in, okay?"

"Will he come for me?" she asked.

She sounded scared, and Garret swore to himself—as he had a hundred times since he'd learned of her attack—that he was going to drive a stake into Asmund's heart for what he'd done.

"I don't know," he murmured, so he wouldn't scare her worse. But something deep inside of him said Asmund wasn't done with Dawn.

Garret had been in the hospital that night, standing in the darkest corner of Dawn's room, watching her as she slept off the effects of the blood transfusion and the pain meds. He'd been waiting for Asmund to come for her, a wooden stake resting in his back pocket for his maker. Dawn didn't know it, but he'd watched her house, too, standing in the shadows...ready. And when he left to hunt his origin, he'd posted two of the coven at her house in his stead.

Dawn lifted up on her toes and kissed him gently. Her lips softened as she lingered. He angled his head, brushed his tongue against her mouth just barely. Just to taste her one last time before she returned to her life.

She didn't understand yet, but war had been declared the second Asmund's teeth had pierced her skin.

Unsteadily, Dawn meandered to her little beat-up Mazda, looking back at him twice with the cutest fucking shy smile he'd ever witnessed. He couldn't believe she was his.

Asmund thought he would use her to get to Garret, but he was mistaken. Garret had been fine to live on the opposite side of the world from his maker, but then he'd come after Dawn and awakened the Destroyer that had been sleeping deep inside of him. With that one bite to her neck, Asmund the Dark had signed his own death warrant.

Dawn drove away with a wave and a smile so beautiful it froze the breath in his chest.

"What do you want to do?" Aric asked from right behind him.

Garret sighed and shoved his hands in the pockets of his sweats, dragging them even lower down his hips. "What would you do if Sadey was being hunted?"

For a few moments, Aric was silent. "I'm calling a coven meeting tonight," he murmured low.

"It's my fight."

"It's not. If Arabella was here, hunting my mate, you wouldn't hesitate at my back, would you?"

"No, King."

Aric clapped him on the back, his eyes flashing with anger. "In hurting Dawn, your origin has directly attacked my coven. The stake is yours, but we will be there for the final death."

Accepting his king's wishes, Garret tucked his chin to his chest.

Right now, his maker was slithering into some dark crevice to sleep for the day. The sun peeked over the field in front of the house and cast a beam of dim light onto the porch, singing Garret's bare foot. Wincing at the pain, Garret stepped back into the shadows of the house and gave one last longing glance to the rising sun.

Asmund had taken daylight from him, but he would not take his Dawn.

FIVE

Red or black? Dawn held up the strappy red dress again and frowned at her reflection in the full-length mirror that hung from her bedroom door. Whatever had possessed her to purchase the same dress in two colors was beyond her. Just for fun, she quickly typed in *What are Vikings' favorite colors?* onto the search engine of her glowing laptop, but with no satisfactory results.

Geir the Destroyer. What a sexy-ass name. Oh, she bet he was a warrior. She could just imagine him in the layers of simple cloth and furs like the pictures she'd spent half the day researching. Modern day Garret wore simple colors, too, and sweaters and shirts without logos. And nice jeans—the ones that cost more than she could earn in tips on an entire weekend. Modern-day Garret looked like one of those sexy billboard models with the fit physique, carefully messy dark hair, and bright green eyes. Well, when he wasn't hungry and they were black as pitch. At least she'd always thought him to look like a model—perfect in every way and intimidating as hell—until last night when she'd laid eyes on his scars and battle-hardened body. She liked this side of him—the real side. Garret Westergaard was a destroyer all right…a destroyer of ovaries.

Everything she'd learned had shocked her to the core. She'd fancied them best friends before, but he'd kept so many secrets about who he really was. A part of her was frustrated he'd maintained that wall for the last four months, but another part of her was now infinitely intrigued by the many layers of Garret. A Viking. Huh. She wished he would cut his hair shorter on the sides so she could make sense of his tattoos.

There was a knock on the front door and Mom yelled, "Dawn, get that!"

Since her knee had gone, Mom had refused to get up from icing it on the couch for just about everyone but Mr. Yin from the Chinese restaurant down the street. When she ordered delivery from there, she dressed up. Dawn was pretty sure Mom had a huge crush on the soft-spoken restaurant owner. He was ten years younger than Mom, but she swore age was just a number in the bedroom. Mom had no filter, sure, but Dawn was beginning to think she was onto something. Garret the Panty Destroyer was an immortal vampire, and yet Dawn had only just celebrated her twenty-sixth birthday with a taco and guacamole party—yes, they were a thing.

Dawn made her way through the old, creaking house she grew up in and grabbed the certified Ash wood stake she'd rush-ordered online the day after Asmund played bitey-bitey-asshole on her neck. She, Dawn Leanne Reed, was nobody's victim.

Might sound petty, but she'd already carved Asmund's name on it in bubble letters and superglued black glitter into the carving to make his name stand out. She was craftsy, and not even her weapons of death and destruction were safe from her glitter bombs.

Dawn held it up in the air like she'd seen on the two B-rated horror movies she'd rented from Bud's Videos and Beer Barn this week. And when she was ready to call on her inner vampire huntress, she flung open the door and screeched a battle cry.

Sadey stood in the waning evening light with a startled look on her face.

The scream died in Dawn's throat.

From behind her, Mom demanded, "What in tarnation are you doing, child of mine?"

Dawn hunched her shoulders and spun. Mom was leaning heavily on the entryway wall aiming a giant bazooka water gun at Sadey. "That ain't the way you hold a stake! You hide it first and surprise 'em with it in the heart."

When Sadey snickered on the porch, Dawn's cheeks flushed with heat. "At least I'm defending this house with more than a water gun!"

Mom pulled the trigger and squirted Dawn's shirt. "For sassing me, Dawn Leanne. It's holy water!" With that, Mom limped back to her seat on the couch.

"Come on in," Dawn rushed out, embarrassed.

Sadey's blue eyes sparked with amusement as she stepped inside.

"Mom, this is Sadey. Sadey..." Dawn waved to where Mom was pumping the action on the water gun like she was about to go to war. Dawn sighed heavily. "This is my mom."

"Sadey the snow leopard shifter. I saw you all over the news when you registered to the Winterset Coven. That, and Dawn talks about you all the time. If I didn't think my kid had a hard-on for that sexy dark-headed morsel in the coven, I'd say she had a crush on you."

"Mom!" Dawn clipped out.

"She don't have many friends outside of the vamp house. You girls want me to order some Chinese take-out? I gotta man who probably has the tastiest eggroll in the world." Mom waggled her eyebrows like a perv, and mortified, Dawn dragged Sadey by the hand to her bedroom at the back of the house. Over her shoulder, she called, "I'm moving out again!"

"Good!" Mom said. "You need to stop coddling me and besides, that'll give me some private time with Mr. Yin without you lookin' at me all judgmental."

Dawn scrunched up her face and shut the door at the vision of Mom and Mr. Yin fooling around.

"I think I love your mom," Sadey punched out through her giggles.

Dawn glared at the door. "Yeah, she thinks she's a hoot." Looking around her childhood bedroom, she drawled out, "Uuuuh, sorry my room looks like a unicorn took a rainbow shit in here. I just moved back in to help my mom with bills, and I've been too busy to fix up the old room."

Sadey picked up an old dust-covered trophy. "Is this seriously a first place for curling?"

"It's a sport! And I wasn't super athletic in school so when it came to extra curriculars, I got creative."

Sadey sat heavily on her neon green office chair and spun slowly. "I got tired of hanging around outside like some peeping-tom stalker. That's Garret's gig, not mine."

"What? You've been standing outside my house?"

"Yeah, Project Dawn Patrol has been in full effect since the attack. Garret has me watching this place during the day while he's sleeping and unable to protect you. Like Asmund could get to you during the day. He might be ancient, but he's still a vamp and will go up in flames in sunlight. Garret doesn't want to take any chances though. Those dresses are hot." She pointed to the outfits laid out on the bed. "Go with the black one tonight. It'll make your eyes pop, and Garret won't be able to keep his hands off you."

Dawn just stood there with her mouth hanging

open wide enough to catch flies. "Wait, go back. Wh-who watches me at night?"

"Mostly Garret. You should get better curtains. When he's out hunting Ass-munch, he usually puts Shane and Evan out in front of your house. Also, we are really gonna have to work on your vamp-staking skills. You held your weapon like a limp noodle, and is that glitter?" Sadey pointed to the sparkle-adorned stake hanging limply from Dawn's hand.

Dawn slowly hid it behind her back. "No?"

"Want to hear a secret that I've been dying to tell you all day?"

"Um, okay."

"Aric has called a coven meeting."

Oh, that sounded bad. Coven meetings didn't happen often, and it was usually about something unsavory. "A meeting about what?"

"We're going a-huntin' on your behalf."

"Mine?" Dawn's head was spinning. "But Aric calls me a feeder."

"Not anymore. This morning my supersonic shifter hearing was on point, and I heard Garret call you his."

"His what?"

"You know. His woman, his lover, his queen, his to defend, protect, avenge. The coven is going to war with his origin to back him up. To back you up."

"That's terrible! Why do you sound so excited about this, Sadey? Asmund is terrifying." She didn't want any of the Winterset Coven to get hurt or worse on her behalf.

The smile slipped from Sadey's lips, and quietly she said, "Garret's already been hunting him, Dawn. The night we found out about your attack… I've never seen Garret like that. He raged and filled the entire coven house with something awful and dark. I couldn't even fucking breathe, Dawn. Aric laid down an order for Garret not to hunt Asmund while the police were sitting outside watching us so closely, but he ignored it. Ignored an order, Dawn. From his king. After tonight, Garret won't be hunting alone anymore, so yeah, this is a really good thing because the coven can't lose him. And we can't lose you. Asmund is ancient and powerful, sure, but our boys are loyal and lethal. He has a better shot at ending Asmund and keeping you safe with the coven at his back."

"But maybe Asmund made his point and won't come back for me," Dawn whispered, desperate to deny she was still a target.

Sadey canted her head, and her eyes grew sad. "He can't take the chance on losing you, too. Asmund has taken from him before."

Dawn frowned. "This is different from when Asmund Turned Garret."

"No, you don't understand," Sadey murmured. "Asmund killed Torunn. If Garret thinks this is a repeat of history, then I trust him, and so does Aric. And for your own safety, you should trust him, too."

Dawn sat heavily on the edge of the bed and stared down at the stake in her hand. She'd bought it because she didn't feel safe anymore, but a huge part of her had really wished the nightmare was over. Her eyes burned as she felt crushed under the weight of the avalanche tumbling down on top of her. The attack, finding out about Garret's past, about his great love, and now this? Torunn hadn't moved on as Garret had told her. She'd been killed by the same man who'd nearly drained Dawn dry.

And on top of all of that, Dawn's feelings for Garret had deepened infinitely during their night together. There was no running from this. There was only enduring it until she could see light again, because Garret had said she was his.

And down to her soul, she felt the same about him.

SIX

Sadey jerked her head to the left and stopped the porch swing from rocking underneath them. Immediately, Dawn was on alert. Sadey's senses were insanely heightened, and it took several seconds before the mass of bats appeared out of the evening shadows. There was such power in their motion, thousands of bats screeching and flapping in a swirling dance, and then Garret was there when the bats and purple smoke dissipated. He hadn't ever allowed her to see him in that form before.

Sadey squeezed Dawn's knee and told her, "I'll see you later." The snow leopard shifter rose from her seat and walked across the lawn with inhuman grace. She waved just before she got behind the wheel of her black Jetta.

Garret strode straight for her, his long legs making quick progress across her yard. She stood slowly as she watched him approach. He wore a black sweater that clung to his broad shoulders and cut his deep V-figure perfectly. The dark color made his skin look even paler. His jeans were dark and sat on his hips just right. His eyes were still the color of his sweater, but his lips were curved up in a stunning, if slight, smile that nearly knocked her backward. His stride lengthened as he reached the porch where he took the stairs two at a time, and then he was there, pulling her against his chest, resting his cheek against her hair as she clung to his shirt. God, she'd missed him, and it had only been a day.

Was that his lips in her hair? He was rocking them gently, and for some unknown reason, Dawn felt like crying. Her heart had been pulled this way and that so much over the last few days, but this right here felt right. Just a hug, and Garret made everything okay. He wouldn't let Asmund hurt her, she just knew it.

"You look beautiful," he whispered against her ear, running his fingertips along the black fabric over her waist.

"Good enough to eat?" she teased.

Garret eased back and dipped his gaze to her thighs, then flicked those black, hungry eyes back up to hers. "Yeah," he murmured through a devilish smile.

And right about now she was cursing the fact she lived with her mom. All her thirsty body wanted to do was pull him inside and make him follow through with that threat. Especially now as Garret went serious and gave his attention to her lips. He lifted her hands and intertwined his fingers with hers before stepping closer. "I like that I don't have to stop myself anymore."

Dawn gulped and nodded dumbly. She was glad, too, only she couldn't find the words to say that as eloquently as he had.

He leaned in and then stopped a couple of inches from her lips. "Are you scared of me?"

"Never," she whispered. The answer didn't really make sense to his question, but he smiled as if he understood.

Garret pulled her hands to his waist, then cupped the side of her neck as he eased his mouth onto hers.

And as his lips moved gently against hers, he pressed his thumb down onto her pulse. Oh, she knew what he could feel. Her heart was pounding a hundred miles a minute just being this close to the man who consumed her.

The heartbreak was done, and he wasn't pushing her away anymore. He was letting her in, letting her touch him, letting her affect him. *His.* He'd told his king she was his.

Dawn pressed her body along his until she could feel the chill of his skin seeping from beneath his sweater. She wanted to touch, so she snuck her fingertips under his shirt and ran the flats of her palms up his washboard stomach. Curiously, Garret shivered and disconnected their kiss in a rush. He closed his eyes again and smiled as she dragged her fingers back down his abs.

"You're so warm," he said, barely audibly.

Garret felt like a stone statue, but not. He was cold and strong, but his torso moved with his shallow breaths, and his skin was soft above the curves of his muscles. Dawn would never get tired of this. She ran her nail lightly over the top of the waist of his jeans and bit her bottom lip to hide her smile at his reaction. His steady breath quickened to a pant, and his grip on her neck tightened just slightly. Oh he could snap her neck with no effort, but he wouldn't. She trusted him with everything in her. He'd built that trust slowly with being gentle when he fed, and caring when he spoke to her.

"You're hungry," she whispered.

He dipped his chin, his onyx eyes troubled. "Don't want to eat until I know you are okay."

Dawn slid one hand around his back and along the length of his longest scar. "I feel fine, and I don't want you hungry while we're on our date." She ran the pad of her thumb across his cheek. "I miss the green in your eyes."

Garret caught her wrist. "You mean you miss the human in my eyes."

There was pain in his voice, so she hugged him tight, up on her tiptoes so she could rest her chin on his strong shoulder. "No, I mean I miss the color that tells me you are okay and happy. The black says you're uncomfortable, and I can't go the entire night looking at you, thinking I could make this better for you."

"I hear a heartbeat in your house," he said low, so

close to her ear his lips brushed her sensitive lobe and just about buckled her knees.

"My mom's home."

"I want to meet her, but not like this."

Mom's approval meant a lot to her. Dawn had no doubt she would adore Garret, but maybe not with demon-black eyes and a mega-boner the first time they met.

She could drag his sexy ass to the rickety old treehouse out back, but it probably wouldn't hold their weight, especially if they were humping…and she definitely planned on humping. They could do it in the back seat of his car, but then she remembered he flew here like the badass vampire he was. Her car was definitely too small to do anything fun in the back seat unless they somehow shrunk themselves to the size of fairies.

"You're pouting," Garret said in an amused tone as he brushed his thumb over her lip.

Indeed, she was. Because diddle-time was not imminent, and her hormones were buzzing like a pissed-off beehive.

"I'm hungry," she muttered. For a naked party.

"Well, come on then. I'll be fine tonight. I have

plans, and we're going to be late."

"Plans?" she asked hopefully as he led her by the hand down the porch stairs.

Movement in the shadows caught her attention. Shane and Evan stepped out from the woods with somber looks on their faces. Shane was third in the coven and had always been nice to her, while Evan, the sandy-haired muscle man was the strong silent type. She hadn't even realized they were there until now.

Garret lifted his chin in a mannish greeting, and Dawn wiggled her fingers in a wave. She withdrew her keys from her purse but then hesitated. Three giant vampires plus her in the car was going to be a tight squeeze, and she wasn't exactly excited about doing a double date with two straight dudes, but okay. If Garret thought that was safest, she trusted his judgement.

She hit the unlock button, and her car beeped once, but Garret turned suddenly and lifted her off the ground, spun her around so fast her heart went into her clenched butt-cheeks. The screech of bats filled the air. Dawn screamed as purple smoke engulfed her, but after a breathtaking second that felt like going straight down on a roller coaster, the smoke cleared and the bats thinned as they flew this way and that. Garret was gone, but she could still feel his grasp. When she could see through the chaos, Mom's house was far below, nestled in trees that looked like little Legos.

She was flying.

Dawn fought the urge to scream again. Garret had her. His strong grip was steady, and the flight was smooth despite the furious flapping of bats all around her. Her breath was stolen the second she saw the lights of Winterset below them. It was a small town, but was so beautiful from way up here. And then they were plummeting toward Jefferson Street. Her stomach rocketed into her throat with their speed, and she yelped as they neared the ground, but she didn't hit like she'd expected. Instead, she simply stopped moving and Garret's form appeared around her, ghostlike at first, but solidifying as the bats and smoke disappeared into him.

He held her cradled against his chest with a sharp-fanged grin. Carefully, he set her on her feet and steadied her by the arms when she swayed on her high heels. Her dress had worked its way up her thighs, so she pushed the hem south again. And then she patted her hair back into place. It probably looked like she'd stuck her finger in a light socket, but okay. Clearing her throat delicately, she shouldered her purse, which by some miracle she hadn't dropped on the sixteen-second trip here. Trying to keep her cool, she stepped forward on the concrete, righted her ankle after it went ninety degrees, and ignored Garret's deep chuckle beside her. "Perhaps next time warn me when you are going to turn into a flock of bats and fly me through town."

Shane and Even were leaning against the giant window of the Northside Café with matching smirks.

"Ha, ha, yuck it up for the new girl," she teased.

"You ain't new, Dawn," Shane said in his deep southern accent. His muscles flexed against his blue sweater as he crossed his arms. "You're the original Winterset feeder. You keep all them girls in line when we get hungry."

She frowned at the term. She didn't like to be referred to as Garret's feeder anymore. She felt like more.

Evan shoved Shane hard. "Girls don't like when you call 'em feeders." Evan ducked his dark-eyed gaze to the asphalt and lowered his voice. "Don't listen to him, Dawn. He was raised by barbarians." Which was possibly true because all the vampires of the Winterset coven were centuries old except Aric, who was relatively new.

"Idiots," Garret murmured as he led Dawn past them. He held open the door for the café and waited for her to pass. As the hostess led them to a table in the back, he pulled her in close and said, "You were never just a feeder, D. You know that, right?"

She forced a smile and nodded, but she couldn't help the feeling that the entire coven saw her the way Dipshit Craig from high school did—as a blood bag. For the first time since she'd visited the coven house four months ago, her cheeks heated with shame.

"What's going on in that head of yours?" Garret asked after a couple minutes of her staring at the menu.

"I know some of the girls sleep with the guys when they feed. I've heard it. I've seen the kissing and petting out in the hallway. I've heard the dirty stories from Amanda and Erin. That wasn't the reason I was there, though."

"I know it wasn't."

"How?"

"Because you aren't like Amanda, and you sure as hell aren't like Erin. You were shy and never pushed me to do more than feed. You were proper about it all, and we built our friendship slow and steady, the way we both needed. Don't compare us to the others, okay? We're different. Our story is different."

"Is it?"

Garret's eyes narrowed. "What do you mean?"

"I mean, you told me Torunn had moved on, but that was a lie, wasn't it? Sadey told me Asmund killed her. I shouldn't be finding this stuff out from someone else, Garret. Maybe we aren't as close as I thought. Maybe the coven sees us as what we actually are. Vampire and feeder."

Garret leaned back against the bench seat and stretched one leg out, rested his calf against hers. "Torunn had moved on, and I tried to as well."

"But you couldn't?"

Garret shook his head slowly, his eyes never leaving hers. "Asmund decided he would *help* me move on. He told me love would make me weak. That it was already making me weak, and he couldn't have a weak son." His lips twisted into a feral expression, and he ripped his blazing black gaze away from her. "Look, this was all a long time ago. I want to live here and now with you."

"With me, who looks like Torunn and is being hunted by Asmund, just like she was."

Garret scrubbed his hand down his two-day scruff and huffed out a defeated sigh. He leaned forward on his elbows and gripped her hands, leveled her with an honest look. "I'm not the same man I was with Torunn. I won't let him hurt you. I swear I won't. I just need time."

And she could see it beneath the hunger in his eyes. He was worried. Perhaps the weight of concern he carried was much heavier than she'd realized. She couldn't keep bringing up Torunn if she was going to separate herself from his past, and anyway, it was hurting him.

She needed to put this date train back on the right tracks so that this right here—this fear—wasn't the only thing she and Garret remembered from their first dinner together. Sure, she'd eaten over at the coven house many times, but none of those had really counted as dates.

Sadey had made feeder dinners a requirement

after she'd bonded with Aric. She made dinner for the girls on the nights they came in, and it was more of a family atmosphere. Dawn had spent many a coven house dinner watching Garret watch her, and now they were here, in an actual restaurant, not having to fight their affection for each other anymore.

Screw Asmund and his treachery. Tonight was all about her and Garret.

"I got you something," she whispered.

Garret's wicked smile was back. "Is it no panties?"

Heat flooded her cheeks, and she ducked her gaze. A hundred times she'd wished he would have talked openly like this with her, and now he was. "No," she said digging around in her oversize purse.

A sudden wave of nervousness washed over her because this could be a bad idea. It was part of why Garret had pushed her away in the first place.

With a steadying breath, Dawn rested on the table the picture she'd taken of them with the special filter. She'd put it in an antique black frame that said G + D in plum purple glitter across the top. In the picture, she was smiling brightly, while Garret was pretending he was going to bite her, had his hands all clawed up and everything.

She pushed it across the table to him, but couldn't read his expression as he turned it toward himself and stared down at it. His hands were cupped around the top corners of the frame, and when he looked back up at her, his eyes were full of some emotion she didn't understand.

"When you said you had a new filter for your phone that would show me in the picture, I didn't believe you. I haven't seen a picture of myself…well…ever. I didn't understand why you would even want a picture with me. And then I saw it online, on your social media, and I was shocked, panicked because I was afraid Asmund would see me there, and you, the spitting-image of Torunn beside me. I was scared for you and angry at the risk you'd taken."

"But I didn't know I was taking a risk. I just really liked you and wanted pictures."

"And I can see that now, but at that moment I was replaying Torunn's death in my head. The thought of anything bad happening to you…" Garret swallowed hard. "But this picture…" His lips ticked up into a smile. "I'm glad my first picture was with you. This is for me to keep?" he asked, holding it up.

"Yeah."

"I got something for you, too."

"A date present? Did you get me flowers?"

Garret chuckled as he leaned back and gave the waiter room to set down Dawn's iced tea. "It's like flowers, but less romantic and more practical."

Dawn scrunched up her face. "Does it have glitter on it?"

"No."

"Sequins?"

Garret snorted and pulled something small from his back pocket, then slid it across the table. It was a carved wooden bat.

"Oh, it's so cuuute," Dawn said, drawing her shoulders up as she picked up the adorable critter. "And look, it fits right in my hand!" She wrapped her fingers over the arches of the bat wings. "Did you mean to do that?"

Garret was grinning, and sure, his fangs were still too long, but his smile was easy and his dark eyes were dancing. "Push that button."

"A button!" Dawn studied the small-carved head of the bat, and sure enough, it was stained darker and gave when she pressed it. Nothing happened. She jammed it harder, and a long spike burst out of the bottom like a switch blade. Dawn gasped and then stared in awe at the little weapon. "Is this what I think it is?"

"Yep. It's the perfect length to nick a vamp heart. Push the button before you stake or with the bat against his chest, either way."

"You gifted me a weapon," she murmured. "Did you carve this yourself?"

"Yeah. Do you hate it?" He actually looked uncertain, like she somehow *couldn't* like the hand-carved pocket-stake he'd made just for her.

"This is way better than flowers. Garret, you like me!"

Clasping his giant hands on the table, he nodded. "That I do. I'm going to teach you how to use it."

Dawn was slashing it through the air like a stabby maniac when Garret grabbed her hand. "Grip tighter. Don't go crazy with the slashing. You need to get it here." He pulled her wrist and rested the point of the stake right over his heart. "Here, feel." He grabbed her free hand and pressed her fingertips into his muscle until she could feel his ribs. "Between them so you don't hit bone. If you hit bone, pull back and try again immediately before he recovers. Carry this everywhere until this is done." Garret's tone had gone deadly serious. "Okay?"

Dawn didn't like the stake that close to his heart, so she pulled away hard and pushed the button again. She used the table top to jam the stake back inside until it clicked into place, then slowly she nodded. "I'll keep it on me. I promise."

SEVEN

Dawn bumped Garret's shoulder as they walked to the next halo of street light. He'd given her the choice to walk back to the coven house or to fly, but she selfishly wanted more time with him before they were back with the others. Well, as close to alone as they could get. Dawn looked behind her at where she imagined Shane and Evan to be following in the shadows. She couldn't see them, but she had this prickly feeling of being watched that raised the fine hairs on the back of her neck.

Since Dawn was now barefoot, her heels dangling from her fingertips, she sidled around a puddle on the edge of the road. Garret was there, hand in hers, helping her keep her balance like a gentleman. When she fell into step with him again, he pulled her hand into the crook of his elbow, right against his rock-hard bicep.

"Did you learn your manners from being a Viking?" she teased.

Garret chuckled. "No. It was a very different time then. Relationships between men and women were different. Touch was different."

"What do you mean?"

"It was rougher. The women in my village didn't need to hold hands or hug for minutes on end. There was flirting and shoving and rough fucking and that was affection enough for most."

"Was it enough for you?"

"Yes," he said void of hesitation. "It was how I'd grown up. What about you?"

"You're asking if I'm mushy?"

He flashed her a quick smile and nodded.

Dawn frowned. She hadn't thought about it before, but she realized now she had changed so very much since meeting Garret. "I wasn't always mushy in relationships. I didn't need a lot from boyfriends." Garret's arm flexed when she said that last word, so she rushed onward. "I accepted whatever affection they gave me, but I kept them at a distance emotionally. I guess I don't have a lot of trust in men following through."

"Because of your dad?"

"Yeah, and my stepdad, Gary. The ones who should've stuck around didn't, and Mom's boyfriends after that pulled the same stunts until she just stopped trying. I stopped wanting a father figure because there was no benefit that outweighed the pain of saying goodbye. And when I started dating, it was the same story with every one of my boyfriends. They pulled away when things got too serious. Or maybe it was me, I don't know. Maybe I was halfway out already, and they could tell. I wasn't surprised when they broke up with me. I just expected it, you know?"

Music notes drifted to her on the wind, and Garret's attention was now on a house at the end of the block with all its lights on. The smell of grilling hamburgers and the sound of muffled laughter filled the air. Someone must've been hosting a barbecue. The song was a slow country song, one Garret liked to play on the old jukebox that sat in the living room of the coven house. His lips curved up into a smile as he pulled Dawn in a wide circle under the street light until she was facing him. Then he eased her in close, slid his strong hand up her back, and gently held her other as he began to sway from side-to-side with the cadence of the music.

"Your dad and stepdad and those boys you dated missed out, Dawn. You got unlucky with them, but not every man is like that. Not everyone leaves."

She could feel his loyalty, and her uncertainty settled within her just slightly. It wasn't an instant fix to her careful heart, but it was a step in the right direction. For eleven hundred years, Garret had clung to thoughts of Torunn, the last woman he'd had as a human. So much that he had found Dawn just because she resembled her.

"How did you find me?" she asked softly. "Winterset isn't a big town, and I haven't been much inclined to leave and make a splash with my life. And then you showed up one day, looking at me as if we had known each other for always. You encouraged Aric to settle here, but how? How did you end up here, with me?"

"The same way Asmund found you."

"Social media?"

Garret nodded, his cheek against her hair. "You know the facial recognition software used in law enforcement?"

"Yeah."

"I help quietly with that."

Dawn eased back so she could tell if he was serious. His eyes were still dark as night from hunger, but deadly serious. "I thought you didn't have a job."

Garret snorted. "Of course I have a job, woman. I'm not lazy. I work online so my odd sleep hours don't affect it."

"So you're good at computers?"

Garret's grin grew wicked. "I was a hacker for years and got recruited by the government to switch to their side."

"A Viking Vampire Nerd."

Garret bellowed out a single laugh and spun her in a circle, dipped her, and then laid a quick nip on her throat. "I had a lot of time to learn technology, and in case you haven't noticed, there aren't any Viking wars to fight in at the moment. I had to adjust to the changing times."

Garret pulled her up easily and spun her in close again.

"So you found me using facial recognition software?"

"I freelanced for social media start-ups when they began running similar programs and caught you randomly one day. I was just running tests on a batch of five hundred faces, and there you were, face one-thirty-two. I panicked. For a moment, when I was scrolling back through to find you again, I thought I'd imagined you, but I hadn't."

She could picture him sitting at his computer, frozen, staring at her photo with a shocked expression on his face. "Which picture?" she asked softly.

"One where you were at a bar drinking with two other girls. I don't remember what they looked like, but all three of you had your shot glasses in the middle like you were making a toast, and you were looking right at the camera with this smile that just…blew me away. You were wearing a shiny pink top, drinking a pink drink, and you had on pink…" Garret waved his fingers around his lips.

"Lipstick?"

"Yeah. You looked like Torunn but looked completely different all at once. You were just…you.

The one I'd waited for." Garret's voice broke on the last word, and he swallowed hard, trapping her in his intense gaze. "If I had a heart, it would've stopped."

"But you were so smooth every time I came to the coven house. You were so confident and flirty and easy."

"Yeah, and do you know how fucking hard that was to pull off? When I wasn't around you, I was thinking about you. Your laugh, your eyes, what your ass would feel like in my hands, what you would feel like all pressed up against my body, what you tasted like. I mean shit, I've had my dick in my hand for four months now, just fucking frustrated because I didn't want to be with anyone else, but I couldn't be with you."

"Why not?" she asked too loud, pulling their dance to a halt. "I was right there, waiting for you to give me some sign that it wasn't just flirting for you."

"Because what kind of life could I possibly give you? What life, Dawn? One without sunlight, surrounded by supes—"

"Supes, who are my friends—"

"Who put your life in danger. In the human world, you're safer. It's just the way it is. If I could've stayed away from you, you would've met a nice, normal human man who could give you all the babies you want. You could've lived a safe life in Winterset, and watched your children and your grandchildren grow up."

"Why can't I have that with you?"

"Because one, we can't have babies, Dawn. I can with other supes, shifters and vamps, but not with humans. We aren't compatible for procreation."

"Don't call it like it's some scientific thing, Garret. If I need to be a supe to have a family someday, so be it. You can just Turn me."

Garret reared back like she'd slapped him. "What?"

"It's legal. You get to Turn one person."

Garret shook his head hard and loosened his grip on her, stepped back, and ran his hand over his dark hair. "D, you don't know what you're talking about. I would never Turn you. I wouldn't Turn anyone."

Now she was the one who felt slapped. "Why not?"

"Because you would be this!" He gestured to his body. His face was twisted in disgust. "You would be a vampire. Forever, Dawn, not just for one lifetime, or two. You would last centuries until you finally sickened and went mad, went on a killing spree like all the old ones do. Like my last queen and Asmund. Like I will do someday, and Aric and Shane and Evan, and fuck, Dawn, I would never want to take the sunlight away from you. You're light and happiness. You're glitter and I'm matte black, and I don't want to dip you in tar and ask you to be happy suffocating in shadows for eternity. No. You aren't made for this. No one is."

Dawn's legs buckled, and she sat heavily on the curb right under the streetlamp. "But...I want kids someday."

"Welcome to the club, D. I've wanted a kid for a millennium," Garret muttered, hands on his hips.

"So what's the plan with me then?"

"There is no plan! This is why I kept my distance. The only viable option is I stay a vampire, obviously, and you stay human, also obviously."

"Garret, I'm going to age!"

"Which is a good thing."

"No, you don't understand. I will get older with every year, and you will stay the same, looking"—she waved her hand around his angelic physique—

"perfect!"

"At the cost of my soul. At the cost of my heartbeat, and all the people I cared about. At the cost of sunlight and fucking steak, D. You know what vampires eat, right?"

"Of course, I do. I'm your feeder."

Garret made a ticking sound behind his teeth and paced away and then back. "You're more than my feeder, and you know it."

Dawn sat there stunned with all of the obstacles that now existed directly between her and Garret. He wasn't willing to Turn her, and she didn't want to age while he stayed eternally the same. What life could she give him then? She would get older each year, making less and less sense with a thirty-year-old model. Her face and boobs and body would sag a little more each year, as it should, but he wouldn't change with her. He would stay firm and fit, and if he stayed with her, he would eventually be in charge of her care instead of undergoing those life phases with her. "Well, I guess I'll be really fucking awesome at blow jobs when I don't have any teeth left," she quipped.

Garret snorted and tried to hide a smile.

"It's not funny."

"I'm not laughing." But his eyes were doing the laughing for him, and now her anger burned even hotter. Dawn barely resisted the urge to throw her heels at him and stomped off down the street.

The squeak of bats sounded above her, and then he was there in front of her looking all sexy surrounded by purple smoke.

"Furthermore, it's weird that your clothes stay with you. Aric's don't do that. I've seen him bare-ass naked after a shift, but here you are, being even more perfect than I realized before."

"That's my power," he said, but the corners of his lips still turned up in an irritating grin, so she held fast to her grudge. "Aric and Asmund got mind control powers, and I get to shift while hiding my dick. Perfection isn't my gig, D."

Dawn's anger dissipated like a Texas rainstorm. To hide her smile, she crossed her arms and looked off toward the barbecue house.

"Stop being angry. It doesn't suit you, and I didn't mean to piss you off. If you still want to stick with me after everything, we can…I don't know…adopt a baby farm animal or something. A puppy maybe."

"I like potbellied pigs. Spotted ones that wiggle

their tails."

"Of course, you do. We'll adopt one of those."

That did sound pretty awesome, but she wasn't giving up on the dream of having a family someday. Garret felt like hers. He felt imperative to her life. She'd known it from the first day she'd met him that he was going to be big. Dawn could be a patient hunter, and already she was planning on slowly wearing him down. "You're going to bite me and Turn me someday," she said.

Garret shook his head and pulled her in close. "If only it was that easy, D. If I wanted to make you into a monster like me, it would take more than just a bite."

"What do you mean?"

Garret's arms tightened around her. "I would have to drain you dry and raise you from the dead. Let's get off this subject. It's too heavy for a first date."

"This isn't our first date."

Garret twitched against her. "When was our first one then?"

"I have them written down." Dawn eased out of his embrace and pulled her pink notebook from her purse, then flipped neatly to the middle and read aloud. "Date number one, Garret bought me tacos after he fed from me. When I asked him if this was a date, his cheeks went red, and he didn't answer. I didn't even know vampires could blush. Date number two, Garret asked to walk me home after I fed him, and he talked the whole way about what the sixties were like. I thought he was going to kiss me goodnight on my front porch, but he stuck his hand out and shook mine instead. It still counted. He was smiling a lot. Date number three, Garret picked me up after I called him drunk from the bar so I wouldn't have to get a ride home from a sweaty man named Creeper Dave. I didn't make up the name. That's what his friends called him." Garret was smiling beside her as they walked, so she continued. "Date number four, Garret called me two hours before dawn this morning and invited me to this pancake place with him. I forgot he couldn't even eat pancakes until I waited for him to order, and he reminded me blood only. And then he just stared at me with his sexy eyebrow all arched up like he wanted to get his dick good and sucked—" Dawn cut herself off and cleared her throat delicately. "Maybe I shouldn't read my journal anymore."

"No, I like it, keep going."

"Date number five," she read quieter. "I really, really, really like him. Tonight he asked me to stay after I fed him so we could play chess and talk, and afterward, I fell asleep on his bed. When I woke up, it was midday. He had tucked me in all nice and tight, and he was sleeping on top of the covers beside me. He wasn't touching me, but it felt like he was. I think I love him." Heat flooded her cheeks and ears, and she kept her gaze carefully pointed away from him as she tucked her journal back into her purse. "There are some more dates, but maybe I was just reading too much into them."

"No," Garret said low. He slid his arm around her shoulders and hugged her against his side, adjusting his long gate to match hers. "I haven't done this in...well...ever. Not like this. I don't know much about dating. If you say those were dates, then they were. I guess this discussion needed to happen tonight. It's not fair that we get deeper into this and you not know where I stand. Where we stand. You felt like mine from the moment I laid eyes on you, and if it felt the same for you, too, then okay. Can I see your phone?"

Confused, Dawn pulled her sparkly pink phone from her purse and handed it over. He poked a few buttons, then hugged her against his chest and held it up. She smiled in shock at their reflection on the screen. He'd turned on the vamp filter and was resting his head against hers, smiling with his mouth closed to hide his fangs. He took the picture, then reviewed it. She was all happy eyes and pink cheeks, and he was perfection that had never existed in Winterset before.

"I thought you didn't like pictures," she murmured as she took the offered phone gingerly from his hand.

"It's a special occasion." Garret leaned down and sipped her lips gently. When he eased back, he smiled deep enough to show dimples and murmured, "Happy four-month anniversary."

EIGHT

The feeders were waiting on the front porch when Garret and Dawn arrived.

It was late, and Dawn was surprised they'd been called in on account of the impending coven meeting Aric had ordered. But here they were, Amanda and Erin, dressed to the nines and probably looking to get laid by Shane and Evan, the coven man-hoes. They were sitting on the porch swing with matching irritated expressions that said they'd been waiting a while.

Dawn waved at them from where she clung to Garret's shoulders like a backpack. Her feet had started hurting a half a mile back so she'd climbed him like a tree. One of those towering redwoods with the sturdy branches.

Gently, Garret settled her onto the bottom stair of the porch and nodded a greeting to the feeders. "Ladies."

Amanda giggled. "Garret, your eyes sure do look dark, honey. Big strapping vamp like you needs to be fed regularly." Amanda cast a shady glance at Dawn. "If I was your feeder, I'd be taking better care of you."

Dawn narrowed her eyes and parted her lips, prepared to spew hellfire on this wench, but Evan cut in. He bustled past Dawn, pulled Amanda off the chair, spun her slowly, and whistled a catcall. "Damn girl, you look gorgeous tonight. I sure hope this dress is for me and not Garret."

Amanda, the persistent little trollop, shared her attention between Evan and Garret and offered, "I can feed you both if you like," with a challenging glint in her eye. "We'll make it a proper threesome."

If Dawn was a vampire, she would've turned into a bevy of bats and dropped Amanda from a tall cliff. She lunged at the mouthy twit, but Garret caught her around the middle and dragged her inside. Shane's laughter followed them inside.

"What a heifer," Dawn gritted out, pushing off

Garret's immoveable arms. "Like I don't take care of you. I've offered to feed you!"

"She's trying to get under your skin. She's been trying to feed me since you left, and I've declined. She isn't your competition, Dawn. Dawn!" Garret cupped her cheeks and dragged her furious gaze from the door to him. "She isn't your competition. You don't have any."

Garret pulled her by the hand toward the long, dark hallway. Refurbished dark wood floors creaked under her feet, and the bronzed sconces on the wood panel walls flickered. It happened when Evan was worked up and angry. Amanda must've been pissing him off outside. She wasn't a very careful human.

On the basement stairs, they passed Sadey and Aric. The King of the Asheville Coven had been reserved with her before. He was like that with everyone—quiet but respectful with an easy demeanor that belied a power that few beings on this earth could match. He could control people's thoughts, their minds, what they saw in their imaginations. Dawn was really glad she was on Aric's good side. At least she thought she was, but it was kind of hard to tell with how quiet he was around her.

She assumed he would do his little head nod and continue on his way without much attention to Dawn, but she was wrong.

Aric stopped suddenly beside her and gripped her wrist, stared into her eyes with shocking intensity. For a few terrifying moments, she stood like that, connected and frozen, as if she'd touched an electric fence. And then as quickly as he'd grabbed her, Aric inhaled sharply and winced away from her touch.

"Are you okay?" Sadey asked him from two stairs above.

No answer.

"Aric?" she asked louder, worry snaking through the word.

Aric cleared his throat once, twice. "Dawn, you'll come to the coven meeting tonight."

"Me?"

"You and…" Aric frowned deeply, his darkening eyes pooling with confusion. "You aren't really alone, are you Dawn?" he asked so softly she almost couldn't make out the words. "You've always been dragging ghosts. You've been the bait. The first grenade. Isn't that why you came here? To start a war."

What? Dawn shook her head helplessly. Nothing he said made any sense, and now his eyes were so empty. So cold.

Garret's grasp went hard around her other hand. "Enough Aric. You're scaring her."

Aric's face relaxed into a somber expression. He stood taller as he glared at his Second. "Two hours, Garret, and you'll bring your woman. That's an order. She's a part of this now."

Woman. It was the first time Aric had called her anything other than a feeder, but despite the passive look on his face, the air felt heavy, as if the king was upset—and a wise human never angered a vampire king.

Garret led her down the rest of the basement stairs and put her in front of him, placing himself between her and Aric. His fingertips rested gently on her hips, and his chest was on her back, as if his protective instincts were kicked up. As they passed under the single hallway light, it flickered hard and then surged brighter. A low, terrifying hiss sounded from deep in Garret's chest. When she turned around, Aric was still in the stairwell, watching them, and his eyes were reflecting strangely in the light.

Chills blasted up her arms as Garret ushered her into his room. When they were inside, he shut the door quickly. He stared at the barrier and then at her as he ran his hand through his dark hair. After a second of hesitation, he reached forward and clicked the lock into place, something she'd never seen him do before.

And now she was really scared. "What's wrong?" she whispered.

"I don't know." Garret's voice was too deep, too gravelly now, and he backed up a few paces, eyes on the door. "Something's not right. Aric doesn't scare women, and Sadey wouldn't stand for it either. She should've called him out, but she stood there smelling...off. Not like fur, but like something different."

When a soft knock sounded at the door, Garret reached behind him, gripped her waist. "What?" he asked, his voice cool as you like.

"It's me," Aric said. His voice sounded regretful. "Open the door."

Garret's broad shoulders were tense so she ran the flat of her hand up his back. He moved forward and unlocked the door, then opened it a few inches.

"I'm sorry, man," Aric said low. "I don't know what was wrong with me. I touched her and I saw… I'm stressed about your origin, but I shouldn't have pulled that back there."

Dawn was resting against the wall now with a good view of Garret's rigid profile. His black eyebrows arched up high and, for a moment, he was silent. Then he said, "It's okay. I stress, too, about protecting the coven. All's forgiven, King. We'll be up there in two hours. I'm jumpy as shit and need some food first."

She couldn't see Aric's reaction from here, but she imagined him nodding magnanimously and walking away gracefully because there were no more words exchanged before Garret clicked the door closed again. And this time he didn't lock it, so all must've really been well.

He still wore a slight frown of confusion as his gaze lingered on the door, but Garret's shoulders had relaxed and the hiss had died in his throat. "You make me crazy, you know," he said through a teasing smile as he set the picture frame she'd gifted him onto the desk against the wall. Then Garret stood beside the bed and pulled off his shirt.

She was nearly dumbfounded by his sexy back, but shook her head hard to rattle her thoughts loose. "What do you mean I make you crazy? The crazy trophy just went to Aric, not me."

"No, I mean you have me feeling like I want to fight all the time now, always looking for things to defend you from."

"It'll be even worse when we adopt our pot-bellied pig."

Garret snorted and sank onto his bed, leaned back on locked arms, and jerked his chin, inviting her closer. He had one knee drawn up, one leg dangling off the bed, and his abs flexed with each breath he took. A leather necklace trailed down his chest and rested in the defined indentation between his pecs. The leather was old, stiff, and from the end, metal glistened in the dim lamplight.

She'd never seen it before. Slowly, she approached and settled onto the mattress between his legs. She hesitated only a moment before she fingered the etched metal. It was crude and lumpy, but it seemed to be some sort of cat with fangs. The eyes were black except for a tiny glint of silver in each. Chills rippled up her arm from where she touched it.

"What is it?" she asked softly.

"Protection," he murmured. "It was a gift from my chieftain after I survived injuries I shouldn't have in a raid. I had protected him, and together we made our way through a shield wall. I was supposed to die protecting him. He said I had the spirit of a wild thing and gave me the name Geir the Destroyer. He made me this and told me I would know what to do with it when the time came. I never knew what that meant until now."

Dawn canted her head and looked up from the metal. "What will you do with it?"

Garret rocked forward and lifted the necklace over his head, then put it around her neck and settled it gently against the fabric of her dress. "It'll protect you now."

Stunned, Dawn clenched the metal in her hand. It felt warm already. It felt like it belonged there near her heart. "I'll keep it safe for always," she promised.

Garret smiled slightly and brushed her hair off one shoulder, then cupped her neck, right over the leather strap. "We didn't give rings." He lifted his dark gaze to hers. "Do you understand?"

The blood drained from Dawn's face as shock settled in, leaving her skin feeling prickly. Wide-eyed, she looked down at the metal talisman on her palm. This wasn't just an old necklace. It was one he'd kept for hundreds of years for this moment, to gift it to her. It was a declaration bigger than any promise ring, or any words he could say.

"I'm yours," she whispered.

"And I'm yours," he murmured. "My body is for your protection, my heart is for you to hold, my nights are yours, and my days, too. You can have whatever parts of me you want."

"All of you," she said on a breath. "I want all of you."

His smile stretched a little wider, and he nodded once. "Then all of me belongs to you. This will be my final lifetime, Dawn. I've waited for you."

"What do you mean?"

"I mean I'll enjoy every moment of your mortal life with you, and when you are a hundred and don't wake up anymore, Aric will end my life. Whatever afterlife there is, I'll be ready for it with you."

"Garret," she whispered, her vision blurring with

the burning tears that filled her eyes. She didn't like when he talked about this, but he sounded so confident, so sure. He had thought this through and was giving up what he could for her—his immortality. Perhaps it wasn't as big a deal to him because he hadn't wanted it in the first place, but this was a big sacrifice. He'd lived so long, and now he was anchoring himself to one remaining lifetime. She imagined such a short amount of time passed in the blink of an eye to a vampire.

It was the greatest gift anyone could've ever offered her.

Dawn slid her arms around his neck and hugged him tightly. She stared at the picture of them on the desk and shook her head at how lucky she'd gotten. She'd known he was a huge element meant to be in her life, but she hadn't realized anything could feel this deep and this right. Garret was everything.

She eased back and kissed him hard, tight lipped and impassioned because she couldn't believe how incredible he was. How incredible this building bond was that she could feel growing inside of her.

She loved him. She loved him with every fiber of her being, and part of her was terrified of taking a leap like this. But then there was a part of her that had been opening up since the day she'd met him, and that part had started out just a dark smudge deep inside of her, but had grown brighter and more vibrant with everything she learned about Garret. And now it was maybe the biggest part of her. Maybe it was hope. Maybe Garret was the realization that she wasn't alone on this earth anymore and would always be there for her. Perhaps it was the bond Sadey had talked about having with Aric. Or maybe she'd been broken somewhere along the way as the men in her life had left her one by one. Maybe Garret had been the cure to make her whole again. Maybe this humming, warm sensation was him putting her together again, piece by flawed piece until she made sense again.

Or maybe it was happiness.

"Shhh, don't cry," he murmured against her lips as he rubbed her back gently.

Caring man. He was Geir the Destroyer to Asmund, but to her, he was Garret the Gentle.

Mine. This man is mine to protect always. Her nights would be spent bathing in joy, and her days would be spent sleeping and protecting the vampire she adored.

Dawn didn't use his knee to lean on like she always did for feedings. This one would be different. It would be bigger. It would weld their souls to each other. Dawn straddled his hips and parted her lips, dipped her tongue shallowly into his mouth. Garret's grasp went tight on her back, and he dragged her against his erection with a feral sound in his throat. His body was fluid against hers as he rolled his hips.

She hadn't worn panties tonight on purpose, and when Garret cupped her sex and smiled against her lips, she knew she'd made the right decision. He dragged his fingers through the wetness he'd been creating between her thighs while Dawn worked biting kisses down his neck to tease him. Garret reached to her back and slid the zipper down slowly, then pulled the straps of her dress forward and exposed her breasts to his cool palms. Dawn arched back and rolled her eyes closed as he dipped his lips to her nipple and drew her into his mouth. He licked her in languid strokes until she was drawn into a tight, needy bud. "Oh," she murmured softly as he rolled his hips against her again.

Could she come against his pants right now? Hell

yes. Did she want to finish without him buried deep inside of her. Not a chance. Reaching between them she popped open the fly of his jeans and pulled his thick erection out of his briefs. Already, he was hard as stone and engorged for her.

She pulled a long stroke of his dick and immediately felt his teeth on her breast. For a moment, she considered asking him to feed there, just to see what it would be like, but Garret had other plans. He flipped her over on the bed so fast her stomach dipped. He dragged her roughly to the edge of the mattress and rested her knees over his shoulders. When she realized what he meant to do, she instinctively sat up to deny him. Garret's hand was there, soothing, firm against her belly as he dragged his tongue up her slit, then sucked gently on her sensitive nub.

Fuuuuuuck, okay this was happening. Dawn flopped back on the mattress as if she had no muscles at all. Already with three, four, five licks, Garret had the lower two-thirds of her body engulfed in pleasure. He was creating a ball of erotic heat that was expanding by the moment and taking her over completely. He worked her clit like he knew exactly what her body craved, eased off, grazed a fanged kiss against her inner thigh, and then moved back to eating her.

Ooooh, he was preparing her for what was coming, but for the life of her she couldn't tell whether she was supposed to be scared or turned the hell on. Right now, this was the sexiest thing she'd ever been a part of. There was no fear, only growing excitement about the oncoming orgasm and the sting of fangs she would feel. She couldn't even imagine the endorphins he would pump into her system, but she was desperate to find out.

Her hands in his hair, she grabbed the back of his head and rocked her hips the next time he sucked on her clit. Garret reacted by plunging his tongue deep inside of her. She was floating on a high of absolute ecstasy, writhing against him, chanting out his name. Orgasm exploded through her in deep pulses, gripping at his tongue. He eased back and sank his teeth into her inner thigh as he worked her clit with his thumb, dragging aftershocks from her as he pierced her skin. The transition was so fast she didn't register the pain until the numbing sensation Garret gave her with his tongue was already working. She was still panting and twitching as he drank, so she reminded herself to relax. Clenching up would hinder blood flow and make Garret desperate. Already he clung possessively to her leg, and his black eyes flashed intensely at her.

When the last of her aftershocks pulsed softly, Garret released her and licked the puncture wounds until they stopped seeping and closed up.

He stood up, tall and powerful, muscles rigid. His pants were open and hanging low on his thighs as if he'd been getting off while he'd eaten her. His face was twisted and fearsome, and his chest heaved with each breath. His lips glistened with red, but her man wasn't sated yet—not after such a short feed. Not after he'd gone so long without eating.

Garret shoved her farther up the bed and climbed over her, spread her legs with his knees. Relief washed through her as she lifted up and kissed him. His fangs had grown so sharp, and she offered him her neck as he rocked against her body, pushing the head of his cock into her by inches. Fuck, he was perfect. Perfect width, perfect length, big, but he didn't hurt her.

Garret gripped the back of her neck and plunged

his tongue into her mouth, ignoring her offered neck, forcing the copper flavor onto her taste buds. God, she loved this. Loved that Garret the Gentle was giving way to the destroyer.

Fearsome creature devoted to her.

Protective creature offering her all of him.

Mine, mine, mine…

Dawn closed her eyes to the room to give her body completely to sensation and clamped her teeth onto his neck. There was warmth against her chest—something burning like an ember. The talisman was on fire. Garret pressed harder into her, stretching her and stealing her attention.

"Oh!" she cried as he hit her sensitive clit. She was going to come again. "Garret!"

His body was water against hers. Stone hard and powerful, but with the grace of ocean waves as he slid deeply into her, then pulled out, never stopping the rhythm, never slowing.

When she bit down harder on his throat, he snarled a feral sound and gripped her neck tighter. He reared back and slammed into her. She was close. Too close. It shouldn't have happened again so fast, but Garret was so fucking good at this. He knew exactly how to draw pleasure from her body.

"I'm coming again," she gasped out to warn him.

Garret reacted by slamming into her faster and gritting his teeth, closing his dark eyes to the world, and now he was the one yelling out her name mindlessly. He sank his teeth into her neck without hesitation like their normal feedings. He bucked deeply into her again, and then he was coming with her, shooting heat inside her, filling her while he took from her. This was the trade, and she loved it. He came so much that it spilled out of her and made a warm puddle on the mattress under her, but still he didn't stop. With a grunt, he pushed her farther up the bed with his powerful thrusts as her body shattered around him. Dawn dug her nails into his back and raked downward as she cried out.

Garret buried himself and froze as he fed. A few long, hard sucks, and his thrusts went shallow, stayed buried deep, hit her clit in short bursts as she twitched against him. As the pulsing between her legs faded at last, Garret released her neck and licked the marks there until there was no trickle of warmth, no pain.

She ran her fingertip across his cheek and smiled

at the vivid green color that was there now. His pupils were still blown out, but the color meant he was sated and back to himself.

"I've missed you," she whispered. It wasn't enough. She should've told him what she meant. She should've explained she had missed the green color in his eyes and the way his shoulders stayed relaxed when he was well-fed.

But Garret smiled like he understood.

And then he kissed her gently and murmured something in a language she didn't understand. She could guess at his sentiments though.

"I've missed you, too."

NINE

Garret pressed the heels of his hands over his eyes and grimaced at the monster headache pounding behind his eyes. What the fuck had happened?

He remembered biting Dawn, but then his bedroom had faded away to leave his old house in Norway in its place. Every detail was the same, from Torunn's herbs hanging on the rafters above and the stack of metal plates near the wash bin to the scratched wood floors he'd carried in and secured one-by-one and the table he'd made with his own two hands. It had been midday, and dust was swirling in little tornados in the rays of sunlight filtering through the window. The cabin had been bathed in shades of blue, and under him had been Torunn. He'd just spilled his seed inside of her. They'd been trying for a baby.

"I missed you," she'd murmured.

And he got it. It was autumn, and he'd been away conquering lands at his king's side. He'd missed her, too. Missed this. Missed fucking and having moments of normal after all of the fights and bloodshed of the raids.

But the second he told her that, the cabin had faded away, and he was covering Dawn in his bedroom. She was looking up at him, the pain of betrayal a deep well in her pretty blue eyes.

How had that happened? He hadn't ever lost his mind like that before, and now this headache? Something was wrong. Something was happening that he didn't understand.

Garret swallowed hard and rested his elbows on his knees as he stared at the bathroom door. Dawn had gone in there and hadn't come out yet. He could see her shadow move in the light that leaked from underneath the door, but he didn't want to rush her.

She was hurt. She'd known he was talking to Torunn and not to her. He'd basically called her by another woman's name. His regret was infinite. It had been a mistake. He didn't see Torunn in her. They looked similar, but they weren't the same, and now he was fucking panicking. He didn't want her to leave because of a mistake.

And why the fuck did his head hurt so bad? It pounded like someone was taking an ax to his skull over and over again. He winced away from the line of yellow light under the bathroom door. Aric had acted strange, Sadey, too, and if he opened up the door to his mind, he could feel Asmund there, so close, watching and waiting.

Watching him. Watching the coven. Watching Dawn.

Asmund had done this. He'd manipulated his mind and hurt his Dawn, and that was where the headache had come from. This wasn't the first time Asmund had filled his head, and the residual pounding ache felt just the same as before.

Garret needed to talk to Aric. He needed to tell him that Asmund had power in the coven house and ask him to send out search parties tonight. Garret had been going out every chance he got to search the dark crevices all around Winterset, hoping to find the monster's temporary lair. Asmund had been smart, moving every night. Already Garret had found two of his sleeping places by opening his mind just a little to the bond his maker had forged between them the day he created him. Garret had learned over the centuries to block him out, to shut down the bond between son and origin, and it was dangerous opening up to Asmund, but he would do anything to keep Dawn safe. He could close in on his maker tonight with help from the coven. If they covered enough ground, they could find him, and end him.

Garret wasn't prey.

It wasn't in him to sit around and see what treachery Asmund was planning.

He was the hunter instead.

Garret stood and leaned on the bathroom doorway, frowned at the closed door. What could he say through this barrier that would make her pain go away? He'd never been good with tears, and Dawn was a tender soul.

He'd waited so long to finally touch her and tell her how he felt, but their relationship had been born during the chaos of Asmund, and until the monster was dead, she wouldn't be safe from pain. Until he was ashes, she wouldn't be safe from the tears.

Garret shoved off the frame and strode for the bedroom door.

Words couldn't fix this.

The best thing he could do for Dawn was drive a stake through his maker's heart.

TEN

What the hell was that? Dawn traced the burn on her chest with a light touch. It hurt so badly. Desperate to see it better, she leaned forward against the sink in the bathroom, but she didn't have a reflection. Shit, it was flipped to vamp mode. She jammed the button on the side, and the lighting in the bathroom changed, the purple tone fading from the mirror to reveal her image. She hadn't any guess how vampires had fixed their hair before these mirrors were invented.

Squinting, she leaned forward and stared at the burn on her chest. The talisman had singed a perfect cat shape at the top of her cleavage. Mother fucker. She lifted the necklace and studied the small hunk of metal, but it was cool to the touch and harmless looking.

Clearly, Garret had given her some magic orgasm that made everything in a five-foot radius go crazy. Including Garret himself because that man had definitely thought he was talking to Torunn for a moment. "I thought you said I didn't have any competition," she muttered.

He felt bad, she knew he did, since he'd immediately switched back to English and apologized, but she'd been mortified, confused, and burned by the dang necklace so she had bolted for the bathroom to escape the hurricane of emotions until she could settle on one. Anger, confusion, relief, happiness, more confusion, wanting to murder Torunn's ghost, realizing that was silly, possessiveness, extreme euphoria from mind-blowing diddles, and finally hurt that he'd ended their coupling on such a disappointing note.

Nothing would get solved if she hid in the bathroom all night, though, so she flipped off the light and made her way into his bedroom, which was dark as a damn starless sky and only irritated her more.

"Garret?"

No answer came, but she could feel something there. Something terrifying. Something that froze her in place and sat heavy on her shoulders. The air was thicker, like creeping fog, and her breath came in tiny, mortified pants.

For bravery, she clutched tight to the talisman. Forcing her legs to move, she crept along the wall with her eyes squeezed closed, her hand outstretched in search of the light switch. Her body was covered in gooseflesh, and her heart pounded hard. She could just imagine something monstrous standing right in front of her, coming for her, reaching out it's claws for her neck.

When her fingers brushed the cold plastic of the light switch, she yelped and turned it on in a rush. She was alone in the room, but the air still felt heavy. She scanned every corner, every shadow, but it had all been a figment of her imagination, likely caused by the trauma of Asmund ripping up her neck less than a week ago.

She huffed an explosive sigh of relief and forced her body to relax. She needed to get a grip and find Garret. Even if she was a little miffed at him for talking to her in another, albeit sexy, language as if she was someone else, one hug from him would make her feel all safe and warm and happy again. And no, she didn't care what that said about her.

When she threw open the bedroom door, she was startled by Sadey sprinting by. The king's mate skidded to a stop, her blue eyes wide and scared, her light hair whipping around her shoulders with her movement. "Shit! Dawn, you're still here?"

"What's wrong?"

"No time, we have to hurry. I'll give you a ride."

"A ride where?" Dawn asked as she followed Sadey up the stairs. The lights were flickering badly.

"We have to get out of here. The coven house has been compromised. The meeting has been called off, and the boys are out hunting Asmund. Aric just called me and told me to get out of the coven house and go somewhere safe. Somewhere Asmund can't get in without an invite."

In horror, Dawn whispered, "Oh my gosh. Garret left, too?"

"Yeah, they are going hard after Asmund tonight!"

"But..." Dawn's mind was racing in circles. "Why are we leaving the coven house? He can't get in here."

"Dawn," Sadey said, casting her a wide-eyed

glance over her shoulder, "he already has."

Crap! Dawn looked back down the hallway with the flickering lights. "Sadey, I have to go back and get my purse. It has a stake in it. I promised Garret I would keep it with me."

"Girl, you're gonna have to break that promise tonight. There's no time. I have to keep you safe."

Dawn didn't have her heels or her purse. She had no weapons but the fiery necklace that was bouncing painfully off the burn on her chest with every frantic step she took. Sadey waited for her to catch up in the sprawling entryway, and Dawn threw the door open. Sadey always parked right in front so it wouldn't be a long run to reach safety.

When she turned to make sure Sadey was following, her friend wasn't there anymore. All that remained was a plume of thick, black smoke. What the hell? The sharp pang of an oncoming headache unfurled behind her eyes, and she shook her head hard, trying to figure out what was real and what was in her mind.

Dawn stepped out onto the creaking front porch and gasped at what she saw. Sadey was kneeling by Amanda's limp body that was strewn on the porch stairs. Amanda's eyes were staring at Dawn vacantly, and her neck had been torn out. Sadey was crying and trying to staunch the blood flow, but even Dawn—dull-sensed, human Dawn—could tell the woman was dead. Erin lay face down and unmoving in the yard.

"Dawn!" Sadey yelled. "What the hell are you doing outside of the house?" Tears stained both of her fair cheeks, and her eyes blazed the gold of her inner snow leopard.

"You brought me out here. You said we have to drive somewhere safe, remember?"

The door slammed closed behind Dawn, and everything slowed. Sadey stood in a rush, and red dripped from her stained hands. Black fog appeared out of her peripheral vision, but Dawn was too slow, too human, to move fast enough to save herself. The squeak of bats turned deafening, and Sadey's eyes were big as she screamed, "Nooo!"

Dawn bunched her muscles as Sadey reached for her, outstretched her arms, and clamped onto her wrists as something immoveable ripped her backward and through the porch ceiling. Wood and shingles shattered everywhere and fell to the ground below them as she and Sadey screamed and clung to each other's arms.

The pain was blinding, but Sadey was still there as they were cast into the night sky. "Dawn, stay awake, do you hear me? Hold onto me. Tighter! Don't let me go. Stay awake."

Sadey looked scared, so Dawn gripped onto her tighter, wrapped her legs around Sadey's waist as clawing hands tried to rip them apart. Dawn closed her eyes against the pain scratching at her body as she and Sadey dug their nails in and clung to each other for dear life. *Don't pass out!*

After a breathless few seconds, they were cast back down to earth like fallen angels, straight for an old abandoned barn in the middle of a field. Asmund's black smoke and bats that surrounded them thinned, and Dawn could clearly see their deaths coming. This was it. Sadey had tried to help her, had tried to save her, but she had a future with Aric. She could have babies and take care of the coven in ways Dawn never could.

"I'm sorry," Dawn whispered against Sadey's ear, and then she twisted so her back would hit the barn roof first.

The roof exploded inward and the bats cushioned their fall right before she and Sadey slammed onto the dirt floor. When they dropped the last few feet, the dust on the barn floor clouded around them.

It felt like cold, dead corpse hands on her skin, but Dawn couldn't see anything. With a whimper, she bolted upright, grabbed Sadey's hand, and dragged her until Dawn's back hit the barn wall. Sadey yanked her hand out of Dawn's and placed herself in front of her. She snarled a beastly noise as she knelt in front of Dawn and, together, they watched the dust, smoke, and bats collapse inward until they formed the outline of a man. No…the outline of a monster. Asmund stood there slowly clapping and wearing an empty smile. The sound of his applause echoed through the empty barn.

"Bravo. I should've known Geir had a trick up his sleeve, but I hadn't expected a shifter guardian for his precious Torunn."

"I'm not Torunn," Dawn gritted out. Her voice shook but it was steely enough. "I'm Dawn Leanne Reed."

"Aaah, but you see, a name is a word, and a word is nothing. It's air. You are who you are so call yourself what you like. I've waited a long time for you, *Torunn*." The hissed word bounced around her head, echoing and repeating until she grabbed her ears in desperation.

Lanterns hung from nails on the walls, but in the darkest corner flickered movement. Just the outline of a person before it disappeared again. Asmund cast a narrow-eyed glance back at the corner, but he had missed that flicker of life.

"Sons," he snarled.

In through the door walked three men, all pale-skinned and dark-eyed. All similar height and build, all dark-headed, all fanged. And all of them, every single one, resembled Garret.

The smattering of breaking bones echoed through the barn, and Sadey roared through her Change. Snarling, she struggled from her clothes, shredding them on the way out. Dawn had never seen her snow leopard, and for a moment, she was awed. Sadey had cream-colored fur with perfect dark spots, and a tail that was long and thickly furred. It was twitching with fury, and her ears were laid flat as she hissed and paced in front of Dawn.

Asmund's sons flanked him.

"Out-numbered, out-manned, out-gunned, and out-skilled, I'm afraid," Asmund said in that strange accent of his.

"Let Sadey go," Dawn negotiated. "She had nothing to do with this. It's me you want."

"Wrong!" Asmund yelled, the power of his voice booming through the cavernous room. "I don't give a shit about you, you self-righteous little human. I want Geir. I want him to see how badly he has failed me. Look around me, *Torunn*."

Something flickered in the corner again—the outline of a woman. The outline of Dawn. No…the outline of Torunn. She wore furs and a cloak, and her hair was braided with feathers down to her waist. Her eyes were full of fury and aimed at Asmund's back. He was conjuring Torunn's ghost every time he uttered her name.

Terror seized Dawn as Asmund and his sons approached slowly.

"Garret!" she screamed.

"Garret," one of his sons repeated in a high-pitched, whiny voice.

"Garret, Garret," the others chanted, taunting her.

"Garret can hear you fine," Asmund murmured

through a wicked smile. "His entire coven can. You made sure of that little kitty, didn't you?" He hissed at Sadey and clawed up his fingers. "You called out to your mate. To your king. The mind control in that one. The power. He's the first I've found who is like me, but he is still no match. He's young, and I've had a millennia to learn to control my powers. I must admit, though, you almost broke my hold over him. He is very powerful for his age, and perhaps in time, he would be able to block me out like Geir used to. I would respect the King of the Winterset Coven if I didn't hate him for fighting me. Even now I can feel him and Garret fighting me. Your men are on their knees in the woods, watching through my eyes the terror in yours. It's beautifully orchestrated, no? Geir will watch me Turn you as I Turned Torunn, and then he will watch me slowly drive a stake through your heart. I killed Torunn too quietly. I made that mistake only once. No one heard her screams. No one saw the blood. No one watched her rise from the dead the monster Geir so despised. No one watched me slide the stake through her ribcage or witnessed the tears streaming out of her eyes as she murmured his name one last time. I was alone in my victory, but not with you. This time I'll do it right. I'll let Geir watch before I give him the final death he's always wished so hard for."

"Why are you doing this?" she asked, pressing her back harder against the wall.

"Because he betrayed me! He was my first son. He was supposed to be by my side for eternity. He was supposed to banish the loneliness, and what did he do? He pined for sunlight and goodness like a weakling, and I knew I had failed with him. I gave him everything. I gifted him eternal youth, eternal power. I gifted him the darkness, and he turned his back on me!"

Stall! "So you Turned them to replace him?" Dawn asked, gesturing to his sons.

Sadey was close to her legs, pressing her against the wall, but crouching as though she was going to attack. *Hold on!*

Asmund let off a single laugh, and his platinum blond brows raised in surprise. He laughed louder and harder and then looked at his sons as if they were nothing. "There is no replacing Geir, *Torunn.* You stole his heart away from me. It was fate that you would be re-born so I could torture you again, as you have tortured me all this time. He was mine! I built a coven to help me hunt you, nothing more. They are a means to an end. They are not Geir."

His sons didn't even react, as if he'd given them this lesson before. As if he'd explained in the beginning they were nothing to him. Or perhaps he was controlling their minds, too, like he was controlling the Winterset Coven in the woods somewhere.

Torunn was here now, translucent, but as real as Dawn and Sadey, and she was pointing to Dawn's chest. No, to her necklace.

The necklace. The burn. As her terrified glance bounced from Sadey's massive form to the necklace, she recognized the cat. She'd thought the spots on it were nothing more than imperfections, but they were intentional. It was a snow leopard. *You'll know what to do with it when the time comes.*

Garret's story of the wolves cracked through her head like lightning. So vivid in her mind was the vision of him lying on the ground, bleeding from the bites of the wolves, begging Asmund to kill him before he Changed. The wolf and the vampire had battled for his body. She needed weapons. That's what Torunn was saying. She needed claws and teeth and a way to stay alive until Garret and the coven could get to them.

Asmund approached, his steps deliberate, and as he leapt up and disappeared into a plume of black smog, Dawn grabbed Sadey by the scruff of the neck and jammed her arm in front of the cat's face. "Give her to me."

Sadey froze, her pupils constricting. There was a moment of hesitation as her delicate pink nostrils flared before she sank her teeth deep into Dawn's forearm.

"No!" Asmund bellowed with the deep voice of a demon.

Unforgiving hands ripped her backward, dragging her skin through Sadey's long, curved canines, tearing her arm in tracks, but already she could feel it growing inside of her. She could feel power pulsing, shredding her insides. As Dawn was catapulted backward and slammed onto the ground, she could hear Sadey's snarling as she leapt onto Asmund's back.

Hurry, hurry, animal. I need you!

Asmund grabbed Sadey's neck and tossed her

against the wall like she weighed nothing. The wood splintered all around her, but she got up and charged again. Asmund wrapped his hand around Dawn's throat and squeezed off her air. He lifted his other hand toward Sadey and murmured, "Stop."

Sadey's body froze and she hit the ground hard. She skidded through the dirt and landed a few feet away from Asmund. Her gold eyes were wide and locked in horror on Dawn, and her chest rose and fell in short bursts. Her pupils got bigger and bigger until there was no gold color left and Sadey stared vacantly. Asmund was in her mind now. Sadey was gone, and Dawn was left all alone.

Dawn was choking, scrabbling against his clawed fingers with growing strength, but Asmund was still stronger. He opened his jaws wide, exposing his razor sharp teeth.

"No, no, no," she choked out, kicking and writhing as hard as she could. She didn't want to be a vampire. Not like this. She had to keep him from draining her.

When tears of pain and desperation leaked out of her eyes, Asmund smiled an evil expression. "Good *Torunn*. Now call out his name, just like you did all those centuries ago."

Asmund was blasted sideways as though hit by a train. He rocketed through a support beam and into a wall right where Torunn had stood. And she was there, standing over him, rage written into every ghostly facet of her pale face.

Dawn rolled over and gasped for breath, but her body wasn't working right. Something powerful pulsed through her veins, growing with each beat of her heart until her body ripped apart. She screamed at the pain as her bones broke, as her muscles and skin and sinew ripped and reshaped. Rage fueled her. When Asmund stumbled upright, Torunn pleaded with her eyes for Dawn to *get up and fight*.

"Kill her!" Asmund ordered his sons, pointing his long nail at Dawn, condemning her to death. He disappeared into a haze of black fog and barreled toward her. All around her, a tornado of bats and deep purple smog filled the space, but she could see better, could hear better, could sense evil better. Her body worked differently, and she was on four legs instead of two now. She was going to fucking kill Asmund for what he'd done to Torunn, to Garret, to Sadey, and to her. The animal part of her was fed by fury, and she gave her body to the beast. She stumbled forward a step, regained her footing, and bolted for the soft purple outline of Asmund in the middle of his cloud of bats and fog. She leapt through the air and landed on him, slashed at him with her claws as he hit the ground hard under them. She clamped down with her teeth on his face, piercing his ancient skin. It wouldn't kill him, but she would sure as fuck make him hurt.

Cold hands landed on her back, and she was ripped backward. Twisting in the air, Dawn slapped and clawed and roared a battle cry. Her animal was fearless, which made her human side braver, too. There was no room for terror here in the dim barn, only war.

A loud screeching sound filled the air, like nails on a chalkboard, and Asmund's sons backed off their attack, shoulders hunched at the sound. Torrun stood in the middle of the barn, fists clenched, head thrown back, screaming the awful noise. Asmund was yelling in agony, his fists over his ears as he writhed on the ground.

Sadey was able to push herself up on all fours, which meant one thing. Torunn was breaking Asmund's mind control. Dawn bolted for him, raked her claws down his arms. She sank her teeth into his shoulder, latched on, and began dragging his struggling body toward the smashed wall where jagged edges of splintered wood were exposed. She had to figure out a way to get one through his chest, through his ribcage, through his heart.

Asmund was so strong, he jerked from her grip just as the far wall exploded inward, showering them in debris. Dawn flattened her ears and hissed. Torunn's scream stopped abruptly. In a blur, Asmund wrapped his arms around Dawn tight enough to break her body and sank his teeth into her neck. This wasn't to drain her, though. Her body belonged fully to the animal, and there would be no Turning her into a vampire now. This was Asmund's desperate attempt to end her, to end Garret, but she wasn't helpless anymore.

Dawn bit his throat and held on as Asmund grunted in pain and clutched her tighter. Her ribs were snapping, and this was it. She couldn't escape his grip. Sadey was fighting one of the sons, and there was smoke and rubble everywhere. Torunn was gone, and Dawn was sorry. Sorry she hadn't been able to hold on, sorry her animal couldn't help more, sorry she was leaving Garret like Torunn had to.

The outer edges of her vision collapsed inward and dimmed, and then another rib cracked.

Dawn looked up helplessly at the stars that twinkled through the hole in the ceiling. Suddenly, the sky was clouded with millions of bats that flooded into the barn.

Please be real.

The air around her kicked up and she could feel them now.

The Winterset Coven was here.

Her mate was here.

The pain was excruciating as Asmund's teeth were ripped out of her neck, but in an instant, he was gone. He was lifted up, up toward the stars until she couldn't see him anymore. Dawn struggled to her belly and snarled as the barn was filled with screams and curses and war. Bats clashed, and men battled. Aric had one of Asmund's sons against the ground, Shane had another. One was already lying on the floor in ashes. A long wooden beam had been forced into his ribcage so hard it stuck straight out of the ground and vibrated there. Dawn tried to get up to help her friends, but pain slashed through her like a battle ax and her body wouldn't work right.

Sadey laid down beside her, and Evan ran his hand down her broken body. His eyes held such sadness as he whispered, "Stay put, Dawn. It's almost over."

Everything hurt, but nothing more than the thought of losing Garret to Asmund. A tight ball of roiling bats slammed back to earth, rattling the ground beneath them. Garret appeared, face twisted in rage, arm muscles bulging as he held Asmund down. Garret looked huge and powerful, a true destroyer. Behind the battle, Aric stood between two fresh piles of ash, holding a length of old, splintered wood. His eyes were pitch black, and his lips had curled back in an expression that flooded her insides with dread. Aric was a war machine, just like the others. She'd underestimated the power and the unapologetic savagery of the Winterset Coven. Garret held out his hand, and without a word, Aric tossed him the stake. Gracefully, Garret reared back and slammed the wood into Asmund's heart.

Self-preservation told Dawn to look away. It told her she would never be the same if she watched, but she needed to. It was true. She wasn't the same. She was Changed. She was broken, but would mend. She was stronger now as she needed to be in order to be the woman Garret deserved.

Asmund arched against the ground, his mouth twisting in a silent scream of agony as his face melted away and his body caught fire. It only lasted a few seconds before Garret stood and watched his origin burn to a pile of ash.

There was a loaded moment that followed that was so profound. The dust and smoke settled, the ground was covered in debris, and half the barn was blown to hell. The coven stood around, chests heaving, bloody, ghosts in their eyes as the mounds of ash burned at their feet. Purring a comforting sound, Sadey snuggled closer to Dawn's busted-up body. Garret's attention went straight from Asmund to her. His body was streaked with soot and sweat and glowing in the flickering lanterns that remained. His hair hung to one side, hiding one of his demon-dark eyes, and his chiseled jaw was clenched. His jeans were splattered with blood and grit, but he wiped the ash off his hands before he strode to her and knelt down beside her.

"Shhhh," he murmured, running a light touch

down her side with the grain of her fur. She winced and snarled when he hit her ribs. Garret let off a string of angry-sounding words in another language. "Aric, what do we do? Do we call the Bloodrunners? Their Novak Raven knows how to set shifter bones."

"No." Aric said from where he'd appeared right beside Garret. He felt around her ribs and arm gently. "We don't need to be on their radar any more than we already are," Aric murmured. "I'll fix her. I swear I will."

Garret ran a light touch over the matted fur on her neck where Asmund had ripped into her. Already it felt better, less sore. Her shifter healing must've sealed up the wounds there and where Sadey had bitten her on her arm. She wanted to smile and remind Garret that they'd won. She wanted to wipe the worry from his face because it was done. His origin would never hurt them again. Torunn was avenged and so was Dawn. So was Garret.

But all that came out was a deep rattling growl.

Garret inhaled deeply and maneuvered his arms under her, then lifted her easily and cradled her against his body. He buried his nose against her neck and whispered, "You smell different. Good different.

This is okay, you know. This was the way it was always supposed to be. I can see that now." He swallowed hard and rasped out, "I saw everything. You did so good, D. You bought us time to break free and get to you. And now look at you." He nuzzled his face against hers making her whiskers tingle. "You're so fucking beautiful."

Shane knelt in the dirt and picked something up. The talisman on the broken leather strap dangled from his grasp. The metal glistened in the lantern light and spun in a slow circle.

And now there was the smile Dawn so adored on the man she loved. He looked back at her and murmured, "When my chieftain gave me that, he told me I had the spirit of a wild thing." Garret's smile widened with pride. "You're the wild thing now."

As Garret followed the others out, stepping carefully over the piles of wood and ash, Dawn looked to the dark corner where Torunn had first appeared. She was there, ever so faintly, her phantom hair blowing in some breeze that didn't touch Dawn's fur.

The ghost smiled sadly and lifted her hand in a silent farewell. Dawn didn't know how she knew, but this was goodbye for always. Asmund was gone, and Torunn's tether to this world—Garret—was moving on. Torunn had been brave tonight, had helped Dawn, and if she had to resemble anyone, she was glad it was someone as selfless and courageous as Torunn.

Dawn stretched her paw in an answering goodbye, and then Torunn pressed her hand to her chest and disappeared like she had never existed at all.

ELEVEN

Dawn bunched her muscles, then leapt up onto a tree branch that was much higher than she could even touch with her fingertips if she were in her human form. Twitching her tail, she balanced easily as she walked on the wide pads of her feet toward the end of the branch. It bowed under her weight, but she jumped off before it snapped.

Sadey was waiting, ears erect and eyes glowing gold as she watched Dawn's antics. Her mouth was open in a feline grin as she panted, and her long tail was swishing languidly. Dawn rubbed up her side, roughing up Sadey's fur the wrong way, then snuggled her head against her best friend's. That was what Sadey was now, or perhaps she'd been that since they'd first gotten to know each other. No one had ever meant as much as Sadey and the coven did. Maybe Garret was to thank for opening her heart to the possibility that not everyone would hurt her.

Sadey moved off through the woods back toward the coven house. Garret would be waking up any time now. It was a strange feeling—knowing instinctively the exact moment the sun was due to set. The animal side of her had changed her from the inside out. The last month had been hard. It had been a roller coaster of emotion that she hadn't been prepared for.

They'd attended Amanda and Erin's funerals, right in the middle of the media storm on the Winterset Coven. There was an investigation done quietly by the shifter sector of law enforcement, but the Winterset Feeder Murders, as they'd been deemed by the media, had eventually been declared the fault of Asmund and his coven. The collateral damage had been done, though. Winterset was a small town with a long memory. A murder hadn't been committed here in more than a decade, and now suddenly two happened? Even if it wasn't the Winterset Coven's fault, they were blamed. The battle with Asmund's coven was the last straw for some of the lower-ranking members of the coven, and the hailstorm of public attention that followed had chased them off completely. Now only four vampires remained. Aric had been left reeling, and Sadey with him as she shouldered the burden of loss with her mate.

Dawn had never asked Garret why he hadn't wanted to be king of a coven, but watching how hard every decision was on Aric made her realize he'd been smart to accept Second.

The remaining ashes in the old barn had been collected and scattered, as if the humans were afraid of the vampires somehow piecing themselves back together after their final death. Whatever made everyone feel safer.

And in the middle of all that, Dawn had this feral, barely controllable big cat scratching to get out of her.

Dawn sniffed the pile of neatly folded clothes that rested on a tuft of wild grass. She liked to smell everything now. One inhale, and she could learn so much.

Beside her, Sadey Changed like magic, blurring from one form to the next. Dawn wasn't that good, but she was determined that someday, with enough practice, she would be.

With a soft, rattling growl of determination deep in her throat, Dawn closed her eyes and relaxed her muscles and tucked her animal away. It took a minute. It took an eternity. The pain was blinding and, for a moment, she wished she was her old self again—the one without physical pain in her life.

But as she lay there on the forest floor, naked and panting, she regretted that weak thought. If she were still her old self, she would still have pain, just the emotional kind. When her thoughts got dark like that, it was time to take stock of the heart-filling bright spots over the last month.

The nights with Garret at the coven house.

His laughter, his dancing green eyes, his happiness that somehow fed hers.

Mom finding a desk job at the visitor center and being so proud.

Her growing friendship with Sadey, Aric, Shane, and Evan.

The feeling of belonging, love, adoration, and a confidence that she wouldn't be left behind again.

"Can I tell you something?" Sadey said quietly as

they changed back into their clothes.

"You can tell me anything," Dawn murmured, and meant it.

Sadey was suddenly very busy looking at her clothes, the woods, her hands, anywhere but at Dawn. "My last crew was cruel, and I felt lonely. There are only a few snow leopard shifters in the world, you know? We weren't supposed to exist, and so I spent my whole life hiding."

Dawn pulled the hem of her shirt down over her hips and hugged Sadey up tight. "You don't have to hide anymore."

Sadey swallowed hard and hugged her back. Quietly, she said, "When I found Aric and joined his coven, I was still alone. Do you know what I mean? I was different. I was the only shifter registered to a vampire coven, and I love the boys. I *love* them. But I imagined I would always be an outsider, even if they didn't treat me like one." Sadey eased back, and even though she was smiling, she was crying. "I don't feel alone anymore," she whispered, dislodging two tears that streamed down her cheeks.

A whimper wrenched up Dawn's throat as she pulled her in close again, ran her cheek along Sadey's in the affection of their animals. "You aren't. We aren't. We made our own crew, and maybe it doesn't look like other crews, but it's ours. And it's amazing. And I never thanked you for giving me the animal. I've thought about it so much, but I didn't know how to say it."

"You aren't mad?"

Dawn laughed thickly and shook her head, stared at the horizon where the sun was setting and painting the sky in oranges and neon pinks. "You didn't know it at the time, but you gave me so much. You made me a supe, like you, like Garret. I can have babies with him someday now because of that split-second decision we made. I won't be some weak link in the coven, Sadey. You did that. I was just this waitress in a bar who loved a man I couldn't keep up with. You gave me power. You gave me the ability to defend myself and our makeshift family. Sometimes it's hard to control the animal, but so what? The parts of our lives that take the most work are the most worth it."

Sadey eased out of the hug and gripped Dawn's shoulders, parted her lips to say something, but the sound of fluttering bats stopped her. Sadey smiled and straightened her shoulders, then looked up into the darkening sky.

Clouds of bats blotted out the final gray streaks of dusk. Dawn spun slowly as they surrounded her and Sadey in a powerful circle that lifted the ends of her hair and whipped it around her shoulders.

The coven was here, and somewhere in this wall of power was Garret—her Garret.

Aric appeared out of the smoke first, stepping gracefully toward them, then Garret, Shane, and Evan, one-by-one.

Garret didn't rush to her like he usually did when he woke, though. He stood stock-still and straight-backed behind his king, chin held high as he watched her with sparking green eyes. His dark hair was mussed on top, and he had shaved the sides, exposing his tattoos. A tight green sweater covered his broad shoulders, and the corners of his lips lifted in a slow, breathtaking smile. He gave those so easily for her.

"Dawn," Aric greeted her as he approached.

Dawn looked from face to face with a frown. If she was in her animal form right now, her fur would've been raised all along her back. "What's wrong?"

Aric smiled, ghosted a glance at Sadey, and then

back to Dawn. "This coven has gone through some big changes over the last year. We lost our queen, toed the line of war with the Bloodrunners, and moved to Winterset. We established ourselves in this community and added Sadey, a shifter, to our coven. We went to battle with Asmund and shouldered the storm that followed." He swallowed hard, and his eyes darkened. "Our numbers changed when some of the coven fled, and it left a hole that I didn't really know how to fill. But the answer has been there all along, hasn't it? One thing has stayed constant since the day you stood on the front porch waiting to feed Garret for the first time. Your loyalty made you more than just a feeder from the second you set foot in the coven house. You have proven yourself important to my Second, to my mate, and to my coven. Human, shifter, or vampire, what you *are* wouldn't have changed what I'm here to ask you tonight."

And now it was all making sense. Dawn ducked her chin to her chest and whispered hopefully, "Ask me what?"

Aric's voice cracked with power as he lifted it to echo through the surrounding woods. "This is a vote to induct Dawn into our coven, into our house, into our hearts." Aric lifted his hand. "Yes."

Garret lifted his hand and smiled. "Hell yes."

"Also hell yes!" Sadey said excitedly from beside her.

"Yay," Shane said in a bored tone as he bit his thumbnail and raised his other hand.

"Yep," Evan said quietly.

The tears that had welled up in Dawn's eyes were now spilling. Oh, what a coven they would make of vampires and shifters. One like no other that existed on earth.

Garret approached slowly and held something up. It was the necklace that had been broken the night they'd gone to war with Asmund. Now it bore a new soft leather strap, and the metal leopard had been polished to shining. She ducked her head so he could slip it over her hair, and then she stared for a moment at the precious trinket.

Breath hitching, Dawn pulled the gift she'd made for him out of her pocket and unrolled the thin leather necklace. It had taken her a full month to make and perfect the metal bat. She set it on Garret's open palm and looked up at him just to see the expression of shock on his face.

"You made this?" he asked.

"Awww," Sadey said in a mushy murmur behind them.

Someone shushed her, probably Shane.

"You told me once that your people didn't give rings for commitment, and it stuck with me."

Garret scrubbed his hand down his chiseled jaw. Eyes full of emotion, he handed the necklace back to her and ducked his head.

Blowing out a steadying breath, Dawn slipped it over his head and settled it on his chest, in the same place where hers sat.

When he lifted his bright-eyed gaze to her again, she was stunned at the adoration she saw there. She could almost feel his love for her like a caress, just from the look in his eyes.

He drew her fingertips to his lips and then lifted them to the side of his head to the last tattoo that sat just at the edge of his hairline. There was new ink—a horizon with a rising sun. *Dawn.*

"You're the best part of my story," he whispered as she traced the small sunrays. "The last vote is up to you. You have the final say in whether you become a part of this. Yes or no?"

Vision blurring, Dawn threw her arms around his neck and nuzzled him affectionately as her animal demanded she treat her mate. A soft sound rattled up her throat. A purr. It was as if her animal recognized his soul. Garret thought he didn't have one, but he did, and it was beautiful.

A word from her lips, and she would be a part of his coven, a part of him.

A word from her lips, and she would never be alone again.

A word from her lips, and she would be his, as he was hers.

With a smile over his shoulder at the Winterset Coven—at *her* coven—she held Garret close and whispered, "Yes."

Want more of these characters?

The Ashville and Winterset covens can first be found in the Harper's Mountains series.
These are the first and second books in this series.

For more of these characters, check out these other books from T. S. Joyce.

Third of the Winterset Coven
(Winterset Coven, Book 3)

Fourth of the Winterset Coven
(Winterset Coven, Book 4)

This is a spinoff series set in the Damon's Mountains universe. Start with Lumberjack Werebear to enjoy the very beginning of this adventure.

About the Author

T.S. Joyce is devoted to bringing hot shifter romances to readers. Hungry alpha males are her calling card, and the wilder the men, the more she'll make them pour their hearts out. She werebear swears there'll be no swooning heroines in her books. It takes tough-as-nails women to handle her shifters.

She lives in a tiny town, outside of a tiny city, and devotes her life to writing big stories. Foodie, wolf whisperer, ninja, thief of tiny bottles of awesome smelling hotel shampoo, nap connoisseur, movie fanatic, and zombie slayer, and most of this bio is true.

Bear Shifters? Check

Smoldering Alpha Hotness? Double Check

Sexy Scenes? Fasten up your girdles, ladies and gents, it's gonna to be a wild ride.

For more information on T. S. Joyce's work,
visit her website at
www.tsjoyce.com

Made in the USA
Coppell, TX
25 June 2023

18505886R00163